The Ghost Hunter's House of Horror

Suddenly the enormous crocodile ripped out of the water again. This time it *was* high enough to reach Roddy. It rose so high, they could see every detail of its long scaly snout, every glint in its pale eyes, every mark on its fabulous rows of teeth. Roddy was so terrified that he nearly let go of the door handle when he saw the creature. It was so close. So terribly close that Roddy knew he didn't stand a chance.

Also by Ivan Jones:

THE GHOST HUNTER
THE GHOST HUNTER AT CHILLWOOD CASTLE

The Ghost Hunter's House of Horror

Ivan Jones

To my wife, Mal Lewis Jones,
with love

*Time will run back and fetch the
age of gold...* Milton

Scholastic Children's Books,
Commonwealth House, 1-19 New Oxford Street,
London WC1A 1NU, UK
a division of Scholastic Ltd
London ~ New York ~ Toronto ~ Sydney ~ Auckland
Mexico City ~ New Delhi ~ Hong Kong

First published in the UK by Scholastic Ltd, 2001

Copyright © Ivan Jones, 2001

ISBN 0 439 99805 0

Typeset by
Cambrian Typesetters, Frimley, Camberley, Surrey
Printed by
Cox and Wyman Ltd, Reading, Berks

10 9 8 7 6 5 4 3 2 1

Chapter 1

The Brushes Beckon

It was nearly midnight.

Roddy Oliver couldn't sleep.

He got out of bed and looked at the night sky. He stared at the tinges of purple, which streaked the darkness. Memories kept bothering him – memories of his old enemy, the Ghost Hunter, who months ago had been killed at Chillwood Castle; memories of De-Sniff, the Ghost Hunter's apprentice; memories of William Povey, the ghostly shoe-shine boy who had arrived in his room late one night and scared the living daylights out of him…

Roddy closed the curtains and got back in bed. He wondered where William was now. At Chillwood Castle, after the Ghost Hunter had fallen into the moat, De-Sniff had craftily driven away in his white van, taking the old ghost, Eric, with him. William, who had been very fond of Eric, had flown after the van to try to get him back. Had he succeeded? And was William safe now? And if he was, why hadn't he ever been back to see him and Tessa?

Roddy turned over on his side. At last he began to drift off to sleep.

Suddenly, a beam of light flickered across Roddy's eyelids. He pulled the covers up, trying to ignore it. But the light shone again, dazzlingly bright. Roddy sat up. He stared round the room. His eyes came to rest on his old chest of drawers. A light pulsed from a drawer in the chest, which had been left partly open.

Roddy's mouth went dry. His heart started beating faster.

What could it be?

He swallowed hard. He licked his lips nervously.

Then he took a deep breath and swung his legs out of bed.

His bare feet touched the bedroom carpet.

He began to move gingerly towards the chest of drawers. The light flitted and danced through the crack, lighting the room for an instant, then plunging it into darkness again.

Roddy reached the chest and stood in front of it. He tried to peep down into the crack, but the light was too bright. He was scared that there might be something horrible in the drawer – William had told them there were awful things that lived in the ethereal zones. Things that were worse than ghosts!

He grabbed the drawer handles, then stopped, frozen by indecision. He wondered if he *should* open the drawer. Maybe he should just slam it shut and fetch Tessa. But he was dying to know what was in that drawer. What was giving off that strange blue light.

He braced himself, then snatched the drawer open. He stepped back, puzzled by what he saw. The light was streaming from the ghostly shoe brushes that William Povey had left behind. The shoe brushes that enabled Roddy and Tessa to do almost anything a ghost could. Since William had gone, he and Tessa hadn't had the heart to use them.

Roddy reached into the drawer and picked one up. A tingling sensation immediately ran along his arm and through his whole body. He became invisible.

"It still works," he said aloud. But Roddy noticed the brush was tugging him. It was dragging and snatching him towards the window. It had never done that before! Something was wrong. He dropped it back into the drawer and dashed into his sister's room.

"Tess!" Roddy hissed urgently. "Tess!"

"What are you doing?" Tessa mumbled crossly as she woke up. She glanced at her clock. "It's nearly midnight!"

"There's something weird happening to William's shoe brushes. Come and see."

"What d'you mean, *weird*?"

"They keep lighting up."

"What?" Tessa said.

"Flashing on and off! And when I picked one up, it tried to pull me across the room."

Tessa swept her long red hair from her eyes. She jumped out of bed and followed Roddy into his room. The brushes winked on and off, on and off. Tessa opened the drawer and picked one up. Immediately she became invisible and she too felt herself being dragged across the room. She managed to pull the brush back to the drawer and drop it.

"That is *weird*," Tessa whispered.

"D'you think it could be William?" Roddy whispered. "Calling for help?"

"Help?" Tessa said.

"Well, *anything* could have happened to him!"

"But the Ghost Hunter's dead," Tessa said.

"Maybe De-Sniff's caught him?"

"It's possible," Tessa said

"I reckon he needs our help," Roddy said. "He's in trouble, really bad trouble!"

Tessa thought about it.

"You could be right. Otherwise William would have come here for us, wouldn't he? But how can we help? We don't have a clue where he is!"

"I think the brushes know," Roddy said quietly. "I think they're calling us and will lead us to William. Go and get dressed."

"You mean ... go out ... now?"

"Yeah!"

"But Roddy..."

"It's got to be William! It's logical, isn't it?"

Tessa chewed her lip.

"You *really* think he might be in some terrible danger?"

Roddy nodded.

"OK, I'll see you in a minute!" Tessa said.

Roddy got dressed quickly. When Tessa came back to his room, she had put on warm clothes.

"What about Mum and Dad?"

"We'll have to get back by morning," Roddy said. "I've got my watch."

"But what if we can't?" Tessa said.

Roddy finished tying his laces and shoved his torch key-ring in his pocket. "We'll just have to try!"

They each picked up a shoe brush. A shiver of fear shot through them, from the tips of their fingers to the ends of their toes, as they became invisible and ghostly.

Immediately they felt the pressure of the invisible force tugging them towards the curtains. Their fingers passed through the material and reached the window glass. With a minute ripple, they slipped through the glass and were outside in the warm summer air.

"It's great to be flying again!" Tessa shouted.

They were heading south. Over trees, above the church tower, across the village green and the village shop, then out into more open country, whizzing over farm land, lanes, then over towns, houses, roads.

The brushes continued to glow on and off. They gathered speed. It really was as if they knew where they were heading and who was calling them...

Chapter 2

De-Sniff is Back

An hour or so earlier that same night, De-Sniff, the Ghost Hunter's assistant, had found himself heaving on a pair of oars in a small boat. He was heading across the River Thames. Lights from buildings and other boats shimmered on the glossy black river around him. He could just make out an immense shape in the distance. A cold, solitary light glowed from a small window.

"Stupid place to live!" De-Sniff muttered to himself. "Good job I found that address book of hers or I'd have been stuck with no home except my van!"

He spat into the water as he pulled on the oars. He was thinking about what had happened at Chillwood Castle.

It weren't no use waiting around for the boss, anyway. She was killed Dead. I seen her fall from that castle wall. I seen her drop like a brick into that moat.

He rowed on. Water, lapping at the sides of the boat, splashed across De-Sniff's legs.

"Aw, it's cold!" he whined.

Slowly, he got nearer to the rocky island on which the enormous house was perched.

At last he pulled in to a small sandy beach and got out. His feet squelched through the water as he dragged the boat up and tied it to a post.

Then he grabbed what belongings he'd brought with him and made his way slowly up to the great front door. It was a long way. A dim overhead light had come on as he arrived. De-Sniff felt uneasy, as though he was being watched. But he knocked very loudly on the door and drew himself up to his full puny height and waited, and knocked again more fiercely, and then waited even longer. Eventually, the door opened a crack and a strange face appeared.

"Good evening, sir," a tall man said. He had dark hair, going grey at the temples, a ghastly greenish face and deep, dark eyes set in purple sockets. His lips were thinner than a pencil line and he looked deathly.

"De-Sniff, Mrs Croker's assistant," De-Sniff said boldly.

At this, the man thought for a few moments and then replied, "Mr De-Sniff? Quite so." The man opened the door properly now. "I am Horace, sir, Mrs Croker's butler."

"Yeah, I heard her mention you. But the boss is dead and gone. Terrible it was. I saw it with me own eyes. But there was nothing I could do to save her, though I tried very hard, I did."

De-Sniff pushed past Horace into the hallway of the big house.

"Indeed, sir?" Horace said.

"Oh, yes." De-Sniff looked round at the curving stairway as it swept upwards through great hanging cobwebs, bigger than blankets. He shivered. "Not very homely, is it?"

Horace hastily re-set a security switch by the door, and then led De-Sniff into the main sitting room.

"May I take your coat, sir?" Horace said.

"Eh? No. I keeps this on," De-Sniff said, wiping his nose down the sleeve.

"I won't detain you one moment, sir," Horace said. "But I must go and ... and see about something."

"Be quick about it, then," De-Sniff said, rudely.

Horace hurriedly left the room and De-Sniff looked all round him, at the dark brown paintings on the walls and the horrible carved heads and the thick, dusty curtains.

He caught sight of a picture. It was a painting of a big house. In front of it stood a man who bore a strong resemblance to Mrs Croker. The eyes of the man in the picture gazed steadily back into De-Sniff's.

De-Sniff turned away and moved a couple of paces, but when he peeped back at the picture, the man's eyes still seemed to be staring at him.

De-Sniff twitched nervously and began picking his nose. The man's piercing dark eyes glared back at De-Sniff. Beneath the picture was a brass plaque which read:

Obadiah Quirke
of
Deadlock Hall, London.

"Must have been rich!" De-Sniff muttered. He took his grubby finger out of his left nostril and was about to prod the painting with it, when he caught sight of the man's eyes in the painting again. For one fleeting second, he could have sworn they moved. An icy shiver ran down his neck.

He sidled towards the door and peeped out. When he saw the corridor was empty, he cried out in a squeaky voice,

"Horace! Are you there?"

Horace appeared quickly at the doorway of a room further along the corridor.

"Is anything the matter, sir?" he said. "I was just coming back…"

De-Sniff turned and stared back into the room.

"Yeah, this place. It's giving me the willies."

"Really, sir?" Horace said.

"Yeah," De-Sniff shouted.

A big green bubble burst from his nose. Horace reached into his pocket and brought out a clean handkerchief.

"Oh thanks," De-Sniff said. He gave a mighty trumpet blow on to the hanky and then gave it back to Horace.

"Really sir, you are welcome to … to hold on to it."

De-Sniff shoved the handkerchief into his filthy pocket. Then he backed into the room once more.

"It's that picture," De-Sniff said. "I could swear it was watching me!"

Horace laughed. His laugh was like the pealing of little bells.

"Oh really, Mr De-Sniff," he said.

"I ain't used to this old place," De-Sniff growled. "Not yet, anyway. It's dead creepy."

"This was … a very fine house. Mrs Croker's people lived here for…"

"Is that picture one of her relatives?" De-Sniff snarled, cutting across what Horace was saying.

"Yes, sir," Horace replied. "Mrs Croker's great-grandfather. A very wealthy and influential person of his time."

"Gives me the eejie-weejies," De-Sniff said.

"Allow me to show you to your … your bedroom," Horace said.

"*Bedroom?* Was you expecting me, then, Horace?"

"Not exactly, sir. But there are plenty of rooms and I know just the one for you, sir."

Oh." De-Sniff said. "Might as well get settled in, eh? Now this is my new pad, eh?"

"I beg your pardon, sir?" Horace said.

"Never mind, lead on," De-Sniff said.

Horace took De-Sniff along a mildewed corridor. A big grandfather clock stood in the corner. The clock ticked loudly.

He led De-Sniff up some stairs between suits of rusting armour, under huge cobwebs and rotting fabrics. Wallpaper had come adrift from the walls and hung down in tatters. There were more clocks and swords and sometimes the scurry and scuttle of unseen rats and mice.

Horace stopped outside an elaborately carved door.

"Your bedroom, sir. Will there be anything else, sir?"

"Er, yeah. Get me some tea, will you. A cup o' tea and some nice scones with er … strawberry jam."

Horace hesitated.

"Now!" De-Sniff snapped. "Not next week! I'm the gaffer here, now!"

"Very well, sir," Horace sighed. "I'll bring it to you."

After he had left, De-Sniff rubbed his hands together and smirked to himself.

"I reckon I'm gonna like being here, I am. Yeah. I think I'll settle into it nice and easy, when I get over me horrors!"

He pushed open the door and went into the room. He switched on the light. It flickered, then glowed a very pale yellow. De-Sniff was still a bit frightened, but he swaggered as he crossed the rotting carpet.

"Yeah, I'm gonna like being the new Ghost Hunter!" he laughed.

The room was full of heavy brown furniture – a wardrobe with a mottled mirror, a dressing table, chest of drawers and a bed, which was as big as a lorry. De-Sniff sat on it, bounced on it. Then he folded back the cover. It smelt musty.

As he was bouncing about on the bed, the wardrobe door suddenly creaked.

"Who's there?" De-Sniff whispered. He rolled off the bed and looked round for something to use as a weapon. He found an old jug. He tip-toed towards the wardrobe.

"You come out of there now or I'll … I'll … crack your brains open!" he said, his voice shaking. He raised the jug above his head.

The door opened slowly. De-Sniff trembled as he tried to peer into the dark interior of the wardrobe. When nothing came out, he went closer. And then he saw, pushed into the corner, behind old fur coats, a figure – a figure with yellow hair, like straw.

It's a body, De-Sniff thought.

The hairs on the back of his neck stood on end. Beads of sweat broke out on his brow. He inched forwards until he was very close to the wardrobe. He blinked, and as his eyes got used to the dim light he realized that the figure was only a dressmaker's dummy. De-Sniff reached into the wardrobe slowly and poked the dummy with a finger. As he did so, a pair of staring, purple doll-like eyes snapped open. De-Sniff gasped and almost jumped out of his skin. But the figure did not move.

"Ha! Ha! What a dummy!" De-Sniff laughed, but his voice choked in his throat. He slammed the wardrobe door shut and leaned against it, breathing hard.

"Where's that stupid butler got to with my cup of tea! I can't wait any longer!" he complained. "I'll go and have an explore on me own."

After he left the room, the wardrobe opened once more and a alabaster-white hand slid round the edge of the door…

De-Sniff made his way downstairs. He wandered along a corridor, looking into each room as he passed. Many were empty, or full of rubbish. Others were sealed up and locked – he tried peeping through key-holes but couldn't see anything. There was no sign of Horace. Wherever he went, though, there was a smell of must, of decay, of damp. There were even toadstools growing out of the walls in some places. Something slithered across his feet on one occasion and he nearly jumped out of his skin.

At last he wandered into the large sitting room once more, past the picture of Obadiah Quirke. De-Sniff went to the bookcase. He took a book from the shelf: it was called *Experiments In Spectral Energy*.

"Ought to read some of 'er books," De-Sniff muttered. "Educate meself. If I'm gonna be a proper Ghost Hunter, like her."

He took more books down. They were covered in dust and some had green mould growing on them. It was as he took down a particularly large volume that he noticed a small silver lever.

"Now what the heck is that?" De-Sniff said aloud. He looked either side of the lever to see if he could see what it did. But there were only more books. De-Sniff glanced over his shoulder to see that nobody was watching him and then pulled the lever. There was the low humming of a motor working and the whole bookcase began to slide sideways.

"Crikey!" he whispered as he gawped ahead of him.

Chapter 3

Mrs Croker's Lab

De-Sniff peered at the room he'd discovered. It was a laboratory. He went into it stealthily.

The room had a strong smell of chemicals and was full of stuffed animals, dead things in bottles, skulls, skeletons, test-tubes, apparatus for experiments, dried toads, spiders pinned to boards, a dissected rat, as well as many mechanical and electronic devices and half-finished projects.

"What a load of old junk!" De-Sniff sniggered. "Pongs an' all. Not what I expected! Not from the boss! Expected something … something brilliant! Not this."

He went further into the lab and then saw a large machine situated on a table, next to the window.

"What the heck is that?" he muttered. It looked

brand new. Its main body was a big glass globe. It had dials and a headset connected to it. At one end there was a thin tapering rod which looked like an antenna. It was pointing out of the window. De-Sniff put his head on one side to look at it.

"Must be summat she was working on before she took her dive!" he said aloud. He noticed labels next to switches:

Activate

Co-ordinate Control

De-activate

Spectral Pressure

Plus many others which he didn't understand.

De-Sniff sniffed hard and thought harder.

I reckon I ought to know what this thing does. The boss would have wanted me to. Now I am the Ghost Hunter ... I reckon I should try it out. "Spectral" sounds like ghosts. And ghosts is my business, ain't they?

De-Sniff's grubby finger hovered over the

Activate button. Suddenly, his nose began to itch, so instead of pressing the button with his finger, he stuck it up the offending nostril and waggled it about.

"Better!" he said as he finished.

His finger went out again to hover over the **Activate** button. He hesitated and then scratched his head with the same finger.

"Mmm," he muttered. "Should I or shouldn't I? Got to think about this. Think carefully."

And then a fly landed on the same button. It sat there right on **Activate** cleaning its wings.

"What a cheek!" De-Sniff hissed. And without another thought, he poked his finger at the fly, which immediately flew off. But De-Sniff's finger, despite missing the fly, hit the **Activate** button hard. The machine immediately sprang to life. Flashes of purple energy coursed round the glass globe. Various dials began to turn and bleep. A deep whirring noise started up. De-Sniff dived behind a cupboard, terrified it was going to explode. But the machine went on whizzing and bleeping and fizzing so effortlessly, that De-Sniff finally came out of his hideout to take a better look.

"Whoa!" he said, as he stood staring, open-mouthed, at the machine. Suddenly a blue ray leaped from the antenna and shot out of the window into the dark night.

Chapter 4

Who is Calling?

Roddy and Tessa were zooming over treetops and houses. They were flying quickly – probably more quickly than they'd ever flown before.

"We must be careful!" Tessa shouted above the roar of wind in her ears. "Remember what William taught us!"

"Yeah," Roddy shouted back. "We ought to go higher because of the pylons and wires!" He turned his fingers skyward and soon he and Tessa were flying at a thousand metres. The brushes flashed on and off steadily at first, but gradually they began to pulse more quickly – and as they did so, they seemed to make Roddy and Tessa fly faster and faster.

"We're going too fast!" Tessa called. "I'm scared!"

"What of?" Roddy yelled back.

"The brushes! Where are they taking us? And how do we know for certain *who* is calling them?"

"Nobody else could call them, could they?" he said.

Tessa's hair flapped out behind her and occasionally flicked across her face.

"It's *got* to be William!" Roddy gulped. "It's got to be, hasn't it?"

"D'you think we could turn round?" Tessa cried. "Try it!"

Roddy pushed the brush round to his left. But immediately it forced its way back and resumed its former course. No matter how Roddy tried, the brush would not be swayed from the direction it was heading.

"It won't!" he shouted. "I can't make it turn at all!"

It gave Roddy and Tessa a shock! There they were, miles from home, out in the open sky in the middle of the night and they simply couldn't get back even if they wanted to. If they let go of the brushes, they'd fall to earth and be killed and if they tried, with all their might, to make them turn back, the brushes wouldn't – or couldn't – obey them.

Nothing would stop the brushes. They were hurtling through the sky at a terrific speed. Roddy and Tessa saw, far below them, roads, towns, hills, woods – all rushing by. Then Roddy noticed water below them. Not the sea though – a wide river.

But now the brushes did something unexpected. They began to lose height. At first just at a gentle angle, but gradually they seemed to go into a dive. Their blue lights flashed faster too.

"Hang on!" Roddy screamed above the wind. He was feeling really scared.

Below them all was dark, except for the moon shimmering on water and then, ahead, a huge shadowy shape, hunched up like a massive toad. In the haze, they could make out lights – like the lights of a town or city.

"The brush is tearing itself out of my fingers!" Tessa shrieked in terror.

They whizzed downwards at an alarming speed. They felt as if their arms and hands were being stretched on a rack. Faster and faster they plummeted. And then Roddy realized they were going towards the hunched black shape in the water. They were tearing towards it like a couple of missiles.

"It's an island!" Roddy yelled.

Tessa was screaming, trying to hold on to the brush. The island was approaching at a fantastic speed. Now they saw that it wasn't *just* an island. There was a building on it – a sort of battered, bedraggled old fortress of a house. The brushes dived low over water to one side of the main river.

"Let go!" Roddy shouted. "Let go!"

Roddy released his brush. And Tessa, seeing what he'd done, let go of hers. At once the brushes rocketed towards the house and vanished through its wall. Tessa and Roddy immediately fell out of the sky. They plunged into icy-cold water and disappeared under its surface.

Chapter 5

De-Sniff Gets a Fright

De-Sniff was scared. After he had pressed the **Activate** button on the globe and it had burst into life, he had jumped across the room in terror. But gradually, when he realized it wasn't going to explode, or do him harm, he relaxed and soon was almost ignoring it. He began to wander about the room examining things. He came across a pair of eyes which kept rolling round in a jar.

"Horrible!" he muttered, fascinated.

He was so absorbed in watching them, that when a figure stole into the room behind him, he didn't notice. But when he heard a little sound, he whipped round instantly. It was the dummy from the wardrobe! It didn't speak. It just stood there staring at De-Sniff.

"What's ... what's up with yer?" De-Sniff whispered in fright. He began to back away from it. The dummy kept staring. Then it twisted its head round to the left and then to the right, then back at De-Sniff.

"I ... din't know you was alive," De-Sniff stuttered.

The dummy took a step forwards and stopped. De-Sniff nearly jumped out of his skin. He searched the dummy's pair of purple eyes. They did not blink.

While the dummy was standing still, De-Sniff quickly looked to see if he could run past it and escape, but there wasn't room enough. So he craftily glanced sideways to see if there was something he could hit it with if it came any closer.

"I didn't mean no offence!" De-Sniff said again, when the dummy stayed standing still. "If I'd known that you was ... well ... that you could move about ... I'd never have shut you in there, I wouldn't!"

The dummy still made no reply. But now it seemed to jerk into life once more.

"Security broken!" it said in a high mechanical voice. "Must correct. Terminate stranger."

"Now wait a minute," De-Sniff squeaked. "You can't do this. I … I'm the new Ghost Hunter, I am. The new boss!"

"Security broken!" the dummy said. It began to step forwards and as it did so, it lifted up its hands in a throttling motion.

De-Sniff nearly passed out. He broke out in a big sweat, which made his shirt stick to him. The dummy tried to catch hold of him.

"No!" De-Sniff squealed. "No!"

He gave a yelp and jumped away. "What's your game?"

But the dummy still didn't answer. It kept moving towards De-Sniff, trying to grab him with its alabaster hands.

De-Sniff quivered from head to toe with panic. He felt his own neck, imagining the dummy's cold hands round it, throttling him. Suddenly, De-Sniff climbed up on to the workbench. The dummy reached it and it also tried to scramble up on the bench. De-Sniff began squealing like a pig. He was so terrified, he grabbed a bottle and held it up above his head.

"Don't you come any closer," he said. "Please! Leave me alone!"

The dummy got a grip on the bench and began pulling it towards him, trying to shake De-Sniff off. When that didn't work, he tried to climb up on top of it.

"Oh crikey!" De-Sniff yelled.

The dummy now seized De-Sniff's leg.

"Ow! Let go!" De-Sniff screeched. "Let go!"

The dummy pulled on the leg, yanking De-Sniff towards him. De-Sniff, in a wild panic, crashed the bottle over the dummy's straw hair.

The dummy's eyes suddenly closed and then the whole of its head broke into pieces and fell on to the floor. The rest of its body went into a spasm before collapsing in a heap of sizzling machinery.

De-Sniff swooned and nearly fell off the bench. But eventually, when he could stop his legs from shaking like a jelly, he climbed down. He was panting and his heart felt as if it was trying to jump out of his mouth. It was booming like a drum.

"You ... you're another of Mrs Croker's inventions, ain't yer?" he blathered. "Well, there, that'll teach yer! Teach yer not to mess with ... the *New* Ghost Hunter!" He prodded himself proudly in his heaving chest. He nudged the debris with his foot. Then he kicked it under the work surface and wiped his sweaty brow.

"That's taught him!" he muttered.

The globe was still flashing and whirring. De-Sniff watched it vibrating rapidly. Suddenly, it gave a ting! And something shot through the open window and whacked De-Sniff on the head. He fell over on to the contraption on the table. It tumbled on to the floor and broke into pieces. There were a few sparks and flashes. Then it went dead.

"Owch!" De-Sniff squealed as he got up from the floor. He rubbed the side of his head. "What the devil was that? An' just look what's happened to the globe!"

He gaped round him at the pieces of broken machinery, dials and glass, and then he saw a shoe brush lying on the floor. It glowed for a second longer and then stopped doing so. The other one had rolled away into a corner, out of sight.

"Who threw that?" he muttered

He looked out of the window but could see nothing. He gazed thoughtfully back at the brush.

"I ain't touching that thing!" he muttered. "It was glowing like a demon. Whooo. There's something very weird going on here!" He kicked the brush away under a cupboard and gave a big sniff.

At least the boss ain't here to see what happened, he thought to himself, *and she can't use it no more, can she? Pity she had to go and fall in that moat and die.* He wiped back a tear. *She were a good gaffer. But now I got to learn all by meself!*

Chapter 6

Out of the Water into the Den

Roddy came up out of the water choking. "Tessa!" he coughed. "Over here!"

Tessa struggled towards him.

"Swim to the shore!" he shouted.

They managed to reach the outlying rocks of the island and drag themselves out of the water. Their clothes were wet and they were cold. For some minutes they lay exhausted on the rocks.

"We could have been drowned!" Tessa panted.

"At least we didn't end up inside there without knowing who was calling the brushes!" He turned his head so that he could stare up at the building.

"It doesn't look very friendly, does it?" she said.

"No," Roddy said. "But we need to find out whether William's in there."

"If we can get over those rocks," Tessa said, pointing, "we'll get to the buttresses. There might be a way inside."

After scrambling and climbing, they managed to draw themselves on to a narrow stony path, which circled the house. The path was edged by a rock wall which formed a boundary to keep people out of the grounds.

Water still dripped off Tessa's hair. Her shoes squelched.

Roddy looked up at the house.

"There *must* be some way in," he said.

They crunched along a path, carefully picking their way. An aeroplane flew by overhead.

"Must be near London," Roddy said. "The sky's orange over there."

"London?" Tessa gasped.

"Yes," Roddy said. "We must have been flying very fast!"

Eventually, they came to a small arch, cut into the rock.

"What's that?" Roddy said.

"It looks like a sewer!" Tessa replied.

Roddy's nose wrinkled up as he sniffed the air.

"I don't think it is," he said. He took out his

key-ring torch. Its light showed up a tunnel as it ran behind the grid.

"It could be a way in," he said. He looked down at the lock.

"We can't just break in though," she said. "It's not right."

"We need those brushes," Roddy snapped. "And we've got to see if William's there." He looked down at the lock, which fastened the grid. "Too bad about that."

Tessa bent down and found a sharp rock.

"That chain's rusty," she said. "Just hold it steady and I'll see if I can break it."

She whacked at the chain.

"Mind my fingers!" Roddy cried.

"Sorry," Tessa said, shivering with cold. "L-look, h-hold it a bit h-higher. Try and rest it against the r-rock at the side."

She gave the rusty chain several cracks with the rock and the link eventually broke in two. She dropped the rock and undid the iron door. It swung open with a loud creak.

Roddy switched on the torch again.

The archway ran for twenty metres and stopped at another door.

"It must go into the house," Roddy whispered.

He pressed the handle down and put his weight against the door. It opened.

"It's a cellar," Tessa whispered.

Roddy shone his puny torch around as they went in. From the walls, great gobs of slime festered and dripped. Roddy felt round for a light switch. The room echoed and dripped. Roddy stepped forwards, carefully. As he did so, he stumbled and went sprawling into a pool of mud and stagnant water. It wasn't deep, so he got to his feet easily.

"Ugh!" he said. He tried to wipe the mud from his hands. It smelled like rotting cabbages.

Tessa held out her hand to heave him back to where she was standing.

"Are you all right?" she said.

"No, I'm not all right!" Roddy growled. "I feel sick! The torch is dead as well."

"There ought to be a light switch," Tessa said. She felt along the wall with her fingers.

"Got it," she said, and clicked it on.

There was a flash and crackle of yellow flame, which spat from the switch. A pale light came on overhead. It flickered and made their faces look green.

"Yow!" Tessa shrieked and blew on her fingers. "I'm lucky I'm not fried bacon after that!"

"Must be old wiring, and damp," Roddy said.

They stared around the vaulted room before walking towards some stone steps. Tessa stopped suddenly.

"What was that?" she said.

A low rumbling boomed round them. It was like a thunderstorm brewing – echoing in the skies.

And then, from somewhere up in the lofty darkness of the room, a huge boulder came crashing down.

"Move!" Roddy shouted. He pushed Tessa back against the wall. The boulder smashed to the floor and crushed the ground they'd been standing on to powder. Bits of stone and splinters of rock splattered everywhere. And then all was quiet.

Roddy and Tessa pulled their heads up out of the protective nests their arms had made. They un-hunched themselves and stood up.

"That wasn't an accident," Tessa said, shaking.

"No," Roddy said.

"Let's get out of here!"

"But s-slowly, v-very slowly!" Roddy said, his teeth chattering like a machine gun.

He put his hand against the slippery wall. His fingers crept along it as he cautiously stepped over the rubble. Tessa was right behind him.

"There's another door ahead!" Tessa whispered.

The door was black and looked impossibly tough.

Roddy put his hand out to see if the handle worked.

"It's OK, it's open," he said.

"Wait," Tessa said. "Can you hear anything?"

Roddy listened. He put his ear to the door.

"No," he said.

They both looked down at the large metal door handle.

"What d'you think?" Roddy said.

"I've got a feeling," Tessa said.

"What sort of feeling?" Roddy whispered.

"The sort you get when you've eaten a bad apple … and there's a maggot hole in it, but the maggot's missing…"

Roddy stared at her grimly in the half-darkness. Her face seemed grotesque in the weird light.

"And when you see the maggot's gone, you start to feel sick. That's how I feel," she said.

"This place is like a big pile of sick already! Just look at that stuff running down the walls."

It was true. The walls slithered and squirmed with green and yellow stuff, like a big pimple that has burst.

"Whatever the place is like," Roddy said. "We've *got* to see if William's here."

He reached out for the handle again. Even before it had moved a centimetre, there was a *click*, like a bolt being drawn back.

"What was that?" Tessa hissed.

"Don't know," Roddy said, looking up at the ceiling. But there was no rumbling sound. All was quiet. Deathly quiet.

Roddy pushed the door open.

Instantly, the floor dropped from under his feet.

"Aargh!" he screamed. He grabbed the door handle. His feet dangled over a gaping hole. He looked down and thought he could see water at the bottom. "Aargh! Tess! Help me!"

"Hold on," she screamed. She stood on the edge – the opening trap door had missed her by a centimetre. Otherwise she would now be in the pool, the dark, horrible pool below.

Roddy was struggling as he tried to keep hold of the door knob.

"Keep still," Tessa hissed. "Keep as still as you can."

But Roddy was very frightened and kept trying to scramble up the door to get a better grip.

Tessa tried to find a plank, which she could use to act as a bridge. As she searched the cellar, she heard another noise, a weird noise.

"What's that?" Tessa whispered.

Before Roddy could reply, the water beneath his feet boiled and frothed. Up out of it leaped a creature with massive jaws, full of white teeth. It snapped greedily at Roddy's legs.

Roddy screamed. He pulled his knees up just before the great creature fell back into the water with a tremendous splash!

Tessa turned as pale as death.

"Help me," Roddy squeaked in terror. "Tessa. Help me!" He kept glancing downwards into the water barely three metres below him, waiting for the creature to rise up out of it again.

He didn't have to wait long. A cold terror had come over him now and he clenched the door handle so hard in his fingers that it was cutting into them. He also lifted his feet as high as they could go. An unearthly hush had come over him now. And over Tessa too.

Without warning this time, the big animal reared

out of the water, smashing its jaws together like a man trap. And this time it didn't miss. The massive teeth closed in round Roddy's right trainer which dangled a little lower than the other one.

"Roddy!" Tessa screamed.

Roddy pushed his left foot downwards, forcing the trainer off his right foot. It dropped into the crocodile's mouth just before it fell back into the water and vanished again.

"Tess!" Roddy pleaded. "Do something!"

Tessa jumped into action now. She sloshed and waded through the scum of the cellar, scouring it, for anything she might be able to use.

"Be quick!" Roddy called. "Oh please be quick!"

Suddenly Tessa's fingers felt a piece of steel, lying on the cold wet cellar floor. She heaved it out. It was so heavy she could barely carry it. But she was desperate. She lugged it, dragged it, heaved it back to the pool. She was gasping for breath.

"Quick!" Roddy shouted. "I can't hold on much longer!"

The water began to boil again.

"Hurry, Tess!" Roddy hissed. "Hurry!"

Suddenly the enormous crocodile ripped out of the water again. This time it *was* high enough to reach Roddy. It rose so high, they could see every detail of its long scaly snout, every glint in its pale eyes, every mark on its fabulous rows of teeth. Roddy was so terrified that he nearly let go of the door handle when he saw the creature. It was so close. So terribly close that Roddy knew he didn't stand a chance.

But Tessa was waiting. She had heaved the flat piece of steel up on to its end and when the crocodile jumped, she let it go. It hit the beast right on the end of its long snout and knocked it back the way it had come. As the steel fell, it also clattered down on the other side of the chasm, thus giving Roddy something to put his feet on. Tessa held her hand out to him.

"I can't," Roddy said. "I daren't let go!"

"You've got to!" Tessa said. "Quick, before it comes again!"

Roddy edged across the steel. It wasn't very wide. It was like a tight-rope. He moved very slowly, conscious of the drop underneath him and the creature that awaited him if he fell. Tessa strained forwards to help him. With a frightened lunge, Roddy seized Tessa's hand and jumped free of the steel. He stood there, on one leg, shaking with fear.

"This place is a nightmare," Tessa said. "Come on, if we're going in we'll have to find something else to make a bridge across the water."

"I want to get out," Roddy said. "I want to go home! I've had enough!"

"So have I," Tessa said. "But how can we get home without the brushes? Remember? And what about William?"

They found an old door to lay across the hole so that they could walk over it into the main house. Roddy was scared to cross even that, and it needed all Tessa's goading to make him do it. But as they got to the other side and were through the gap, the door slammed shut behind them, pushing their bridge away and closing the trap door once more.

They found themselves in a long corridor – a dark, slimy, stinking place with strange creaking sounds and bats hanging from the ceilings.

"My head's hurting!" Roddy groaned. "And my foot's gone numb! Let's sit down for a minute."

They sat down on a worm-eaten old blanket chest. The whole place smelled of rotting wood and earth and woodlice.

"Take some deep breaths," Tessa said.

"I'd rather not, thanks," Roddy managed to smile. "I'll probably get lung damage!"

"Come on," Tessa said after a while. "We'd better move."

Without his right trainer, Roddy had to walk slowly. His foot was soaking wet and cold. He and Tessa hadn't gone far when they came to some small rooms.

"Weird place," Roddy said, looking in at one.

"Look at this one," Tessa said. "It's got a statue in it."

The gold statue stood in a niche on the far side of the room.

"Let's take a closer look," Roddy said.

"Be careful."

The small room had a nasty feeling to it.

"I don't like it," Tessa said. "Let's get out."

"Hang on," Roddy said. "That statue. It reminds me of somebody."

"It looks like Mrs Croker!'"

Roddy reached out to pick it up.

"Don't!" Tessa said.

But it wouldn't move anyway. It was as if it was stuck to the stone sill. Roddy pulled harder. As he did so, the door banged shut behind them. They both whizzed round.

"You idiot!" Tessa screamed. "I told you not to touch it!"

The door was shut tight.

"Help me open it, Roddy!" she hissed. Roddy put his weight against the door and tried to force it open. It wouldn't move.

"We're stuck, Roddy! We can't get out!" Tessa cried. She looked round the bare room helplessly. It was very quiet. And then they heard a sound.

"What's that?" Tessa hissed.

"I don't know," he said.

"The walls, Tess gasped. "They're moving, Roddy. They're closing in on us."

Roddy pushed at one of the walls, trying to hold it back.

"Shove your feet against it!" he shouted. Tessa braced her feet to try and prevent the wall moving, but she soon found that the force and pressure of whatever was driving it was stronger ... much stronger than either her or Roddy.

"Help!" she screamed. "Oh, Roddy! We're going to be crushed to death."

Chapter 7

A Nasty Shock

De-Sniff was enjoying himself.

Now that he'd dealt with the dummy, he was feeling a lot more confident. He was nosing around Mrs Croker's lab. His flat feet crunched bits of the broken globe and he kept kicking them under the benches as if he was scoring goals.

"Yes!" he yelled, when one piece landed in the wastebin by accident.

He picked things up, one by one, examining them, smelling them, shaking them. He opened drawers and read notes which Mrs Croker had made. He ferreted around in all the cupboards too, hoping he'd find some more ghosts. He didn't notice the laboratory door slide open again. He didn't notice a tall figure glide silently, angrily towards him. Even when the figure stood right behind him, De-Sniff didn't notice. Even when the figure's bloodshot eyes bored into the back of his head.

But as soon as a hand like a claw shot forwards and seized his shoulder, De-Sniff spun round in terror. He came face to face with someone he knew well. It was his old boss, the Ghost Hunter! Harder, colder, than ever! Seeing her again turned De-Sniff to blubber. For a couple of seconds, he just stood there, gawping and blathering and drooling as if Mrs Croker was a ghost herself.

"*Boss*?" he whimpered. "Boss? You're you're … alive, boss!"

"Yes!" she hissed. "I'm alive! Did you really think a moat full of water could get rid of me? *Did you really think I had no other powers?*"

"Er, no, boss," De-Sniff whispered.

"You fool!" She shrieked. "I am the Ghost Hunter! And when I am threatened, when I am in danger, I can call on those powers to help me!"

De-Sniff's brain turned this information over slowly. He was just about to say how pleased he was to see her, when Mrs Croker cut across him in her harsh voice.

"You gormless, half-baked, snivelling weed!" She staggered forwards towards her smashed-up invention. "You half-wit, you freak of nature, you dolt, you imbecile! Look what you've done to my *beautiful* Spectrika!"

De-Sniff gazed ashamedly at all the broken pieces.

"I didn't know, boss, that you were ... still with us ... boss ... or I'd never in a million, billion, trillion years have touched that thing, I wouldn't, boss. But I was just trying to carry on where you left off, boss. I was. Honest, boss!"

De-Sniff looked up hopelessly and shuddered. A long dangler oozed from his nose and dripped on to his shoe.

She glared at him.

"It was an ... an accident, boss. I didn't do nothing."

Horace now came into the lab and stood next to Mrs Croker. He had a thin smile on his lips.

"Get rid of him," Mrs Croker commanded. "Take him out of my sight!"

Horace's dark eyes closed for a second, hiding a look which might have chilled De-Sniff to the core, if he'd noticed it.

"Certainly, ma'am," he said with a slight bow of the head. He moved forwards and held De-Sniff's arm in an iron grip.

"This way, Mr De-Sniff," he said. And as he spoke, he gave De-Sniff a powerful yank which nearly pulled him over.

"No … wait," De-Sniff yelled as he was dragged across the room. "I … I … want to stay with you, boss."

Horace seized the door with his free hand and opened it. De-Sniff was terrified.

"Wait, boss. Wait! *I got a ghost!*"

Mrs Croker turned on him in a flash. "A ghost?" she hissed.

"Yeah, boss. Tell him to let me go and I'll get it for you."

Mrs Croker nodded at Horace.

"Very well, ma'am," Horace said in a disappointed tone, and let De-Sniff's arm go.

"Where is it?" Mrs Croker's dark voice growled.

"Then can I stay with you … as your assistant? Eh, boss? If I get the ghost for you? Can I? Please? I'll do anything for you, boss, I will."

A dangerous little smile flickered at the corner of the Ghost Hunter's lips.

"Very well," she said.

"It's that ghost … one of them ghosts from the castle. You remember. That old un. Eric, I think they called him. I got him just before I left. I bottled him. I left him in the van, I did."

"Don't you mess with me, De-Sniff, do you hear?"

"No boss. I mean, yes boss. I mean … I can go and get him now. If you want."

Mrs Croker's bruised face, which had been damaged when she fell from the castle ramparts, lit up for a second.

"Yes. Get him," she said.

"Right, boss. I will. Straight away."

"Horace, you go with him."

De-Sniff looked scared again.

"Does he have to, boss? You can trust me, you know that."

Chapter 8

The Spectrika

As soon as De-Sniff had got the jar containing Eric from his scruffy van, he and Horace got back into the rowing boat. Horace rowed steadily across the river and didn't speak to his travelling companion. This made De-Sniff feel uncomfortable. He kept taking out the jar, peering at Eric, who sat dejected and forlorn inside it.

"First ghost I ever caught was this un," De-Sniff said.

Horace didn't reply.

"Talk to yerself, De-Sniff," De-Sniff muttered.

Eventually they reached Deadlock Hall. De-Sniff walked jauntily along the gruesome corridors of the house, clutching the jar in his skinny fist.

"Yeah," he grinned at the bottled ghost, "got you well banged up, ain't I, you little horror!"

He wiped his boil-encrusted snitch along the sleeve of his dirty coat. When he and Horace reached the laboratory door, he pushed past the butler.

Mrs Croker was working; trying to repair the Spectrika. She had already re-built part of it.

She turned on De-Sniff. Her eyes glared at him.

"You!" she hissed. "You've practically destroyed my Spectrika. The antenna is completely beyond repair!"

"Sorry boss, it were an accident."

"*You* are an accident!" Mrs Croker said. "The trouble you've caused me! Now I've got to make a Ghost Nabber and I'll have to go out hunting again with that, instead of sitting back waiting for the ghosts to be pulled here against their wills!" She swirled towards him in a startling new red cloak. "If only you'd keep your meddling fingers out of things. Where's the bottled spirit?"

"It's here, boss!" De-Sniff cried, holding up the jar. "Trapped like a butterfly on a pin."

"Give it to me!" Mrs Croker snarled, and wrenched it from his hand.

"Yeah, boss. Course. No need to snatch!"

Mrs Croker ignored him and stared with pleasure at Eric.

"These old ones don't have much spectral energy," she muttered. "But he'll do. I've got a few more really ancient ones I've had in storage as well."

She put the jar carefully down on the bench. Then she looked at De–Sniff. He moved from one foot to the other.

"Good, ain't it boss? Ain't you going to put it in your collection?"

"No more collection, De–Sniff. I've got bigger fish to fry."

"What, like sharks and whales?" he said.

"No, you idiot!" Mrs Croker yelled.

"I ... I caught him all by myself," De–Sniff bragged.

"Yes. When you should have been helping me," Mrs Croker said, her eyes flashing. "You deserted me at Chillwood Castle. Don't deny it!" She turned to Horace. "Get rid of him."

"My pleasure, ma'am," Horace said.

"Eh? No boss!" De–Sniff pleaded. His face fell. "I didn't just leave you boss ... at the castle... It was a misunderstanding. I thought..."

"*Thought*? You don't think, De-Sniff. You haven't got a live brain cell in that corroded skull of yours. Get rid of him!"

"But you said I could stay," De-Sniff whined. "It ain't fair. I'm your apprentice. I ain't got nowhere to go if you chuck me out."

Mrs Croker smiled an evil smile.

"Oh, I wasn't thinking of throwing you out of the house. Only throwing you into the pool in the cellar. That's all." She gave a nasty little chuckle and Horace smiled too.

De-Sniff was terrified.

Horace took a step forwards, ready to grip De-Sniff's arm again and yank him out of the room.

"Wait, boss," De-Sniff said, desperately. "I ... got something else to tell you."

"What?" Mrs Croker said.

"About the Specko..." he gestured towards the machine on the bench.

"What about it?"

"You got to promise to let me stay first," De-Sniff said. "Properly. Not change your mind or anything afterwards. You got to promise ... on your great-grandfather's grave!"

"Who told you about my great-grandfather?"

"I saw his picture," De-Sniff said. "You got to promise on him."

Mrs Croker's eyes narrowed dangerously again.

"Tell me!" she shrieked.

"Can I stay with you then, boss? I'll do better than I done before. And I did get you that ghost, didn't I?"

Mrs Croker thought about it for a moment.

"Very well," she snapped. "But if you ever let me down again, De-Sniff…"

"No, boss, I won't ever, boss. Never!"

Mrs Croker gestured to Horace to leave, which he did, silently and rather reluctantly.

"Tell me about the Spectrika!" she hissed.

"Well…" De-Sniff began nervously. "When I didn't think you was coming back no more, I thought I had to carry on for you, boss…"

"Yes, yes. Get on with it," Mrs Croker snapped.

"Well, when I saw that contraption and I saw all them buttons, **Activate** and **Co-ordinate Control** an'…"

"Yes!" Mrs Croker interrupted again. "We know all that! Get on with it. What else?"

"Well, after it began buzzing and humming and whirring," De-Sniff said. "A bit later on it was, something flew through that window and belted me on the head and that's what made me fall over on the Specko and break it. It was an accident, boss, honest."

"Something flew in the window?" Mrs Croker cried. "But why didn't you tell me before? It means my machine must have worked!"

"Oh, yeah, It worked all right, boss," De-Sniff said enthusiastically. "Gave me a right thwack round the lughole it did."

"What did?" Mrs Croker shouted.

"A brush," De-Sniff said. "A shoe-cleaning brush."

"A *brush*?" Mrs Croker whispered to herself. "Where is it? Show it to me at once!"

"It was glowing, boss. It scared me."

"Never mind that. Find it now! Bring it!"

"Hang on then, boss," De-Sniff said. He got down on his hands and knees and started to look under the cupboard where he'd kicked it.

"What are you doing, you great lump?" Mrs Croker demanded.

"It's here somewhere," De-Sniff called. "I kicked it under here." He crawled right under the cupboard and at last spotted the shoeshine brush resting right against the wall. It looked quite harmless now.

De-Sniff's fingers closed round it. But as soon as he touched the brush, De-Sniff felt a tingling sensation run up his arm and all through his body.

"Hey," he said. "What's that?"

But Mrs Croker could no longer hear him. Furthermore, she couldn't see him either. He had become invisible. So when he came out from beneath the big piece of furniture and held the brush out to Mrs Croker with the words, "Here it is, boss," she took no notice of him at all. In fact she ignored him, though he was standing right in front of her. Instead, she bent down and yelled under the cupboard.

"Hurry up, you twit. What are you doing down there?"

"But I ain't down there. I'm here, boss," De-Sniff said. "I'm here. Did that accident in that moat make you short-sighted or something?"

But Mrs Croker still ignored him. She bent down even further and yelled.

"De-Sniff, what the blazes are you doing under there?"

"I ain't under there!" De-Sniff yelled loudly. "I'm here, boss!"

Mrs Croker took no notice. She got down on her hands and knees.

"De-Sniff, you idiot, what are you playing at?"

She stood up again and looked around her. De-Sniff was standing right in front of her, still holding out the brush. He smiled.

"Here I am, boss. Here's the…"

But Mrs Croker took a couple of steps towards him and walked straight through him! De-Sniff, completely astounded, spun round, only to see Mrs Croker peering under the table.

"De-Sniff!" she yelled.

De-Sniff stared at the brush in his hand. He realized something amazing was happening. Something so wonderful he could barely believe it. His mouth dropped open, his nose ran. He put his hand out towards Mrs Croker and touched her, but she didn't feel him at all.

"Oh crikey!" he whispered softly, "I've found a magic brush, I have!"

And Mrs Croker couldn't even smell him with her superior ghost-smelling nose because her fall had damaged it.

"Eh, boss!" De-Sniff tried one more time. "Look!"

Mrs Croker still didn't look at him.

"Boo!" De-Sniff said with a chuckle. "Boo! Boo! You great hairy cowpat!"

Still Mrs Croker took no notice. It was wonderful for De-Sniff. He began to enjoy himself. He darted over to the bench and made a glass jar wobble about. Mrs Croker rushed over to it immediately, thinking it was going to smash. When she had steadied it, she gazed thoughtfully round the room.

"Must be the wind," she said. "De-Sniff, where are you? If you don't come out this very minute, I'll throw you to the crocs! Do you hear me, De-Sniff?"

De-Sniff stood right in front of her laughing.

"You ca ... aan't see me!" De-Sniff chanted. "You can't see me! Pig face! Truffle chops! And you can't find me! Ha! Old bossy boots!"

"Stop playing silly beggars and come out of there!" Mrs Croker called.

De-Sniff walked across the lab to the door and opened it.

Mrs Croker looked up expectantly. When nobody came in, she went to it and peered out into the corridor.

"De-Sniff?" she called.

No answer.

Then De-Sniff skipped over to the bench and knocked a spanner on to the floor. It tinkled. Mrs Croker twisted round.

"What's going on?" she shrieked. "De-Sniff! I do believe there's a…" Mrs Croker tried to sniff, but her smell just wouldn't work. She opened a locked cupboard and grabbed a can of Ghost Immobilizing Vapour. Luckily, De-Sniff saw her. He put down the brush and re-appeared.

"Hello, boss," he said meekly.

Mrs Croker was taken aback.

"Where've you been?" she demanded. "Where were you? Eh?"

"I was here all the time, boss," De-Sniff giggled.

"What are you talking about?" Mrs Croker muttered. "I think there's a beastly ghost around," she said.

De-Sniff laughed.

"What are you laughing at?" Mrs Croker snapped.

"It ain't no ghost, boss." De-Sniff chuckled.

"And where did you come from?" Mrs Croker snapped. "You pop up and down like bread in a toaster! Where's that brush, you twerp?"

"Got something very special for you, boss," De-Sniff crowed.

"What?"

"Got something *really* special."

"What d'you mean?" Mrs Croker demanded, turning on him fiercely. But De-Sniff was enjoying teasing her.

"Something so special, you'll be as happy as a sandboy with it, you will."

"What are you talking about?" Mrs Croker bellowed. She leaped forwards suddenly, like a lioness striking its prey, and seized her assistant by his collar.

"Er ... over there, boss," he pointed at the shoe brush.

"Pick it up, boss," De-Sniff said. "Go on, pick it up! It's magic!"

"Magic? What d'you mean, magic? Only half-wits believe in such twaddle!"

"Just pick it up, boss," De-Sniff said.

The Ghost Hunter's damaged fingers closed round the brush.

At once she felt a strange tingling sensation run up her arm. She vanished before De-Sniff's eyes. But, of course, she could still see him.

"Walk towards me boss," he said. "Wherever you are."

"What are you on about?" Mrs Croker said. She could still see De-Sniff clearly. She was a little disappointed that nothing seemed to have happened.

"Go on boss, walk towards me and keep on walking."

Mrs Croker walked towards her assistant slowly. She was limping still.

"When you reach me, just keep on going!" De-Sniff said.

Mrs Croker did so and to her absolute astonishment – as she came face to face with De-Sniff's revolting nose – she walked straight through him.

"Have yer done it yet, boss?" De-Sniff called.

But Mrs Croker didn't answer. Instead she felt her feet lift from the ground and her head rise up to and through the ceiling of the laboratory. She found herself in a bedroom with a long mirror in it. But when she looked in the mirror, she couldn't see herself. She placed the brush carefully on to a dressing-table. Immediately she reappeared and saw her reflection. Now she took up the brush again and her reflection vanished. Mrs Croker beamed from ear to ear. Then she heard, faintly, De-Sniff calling for her.

She floated through the floor and arrived back in the lab. She put the brush down gently and became solid.

Mrs Croker turned on De-Sniff.

"A good find, apprentice. But it's mine. Don't touch it. Do you hear?"

"Can't I just sometimes?"

"No! Never! This is a gift to me, De-Sniff. To help me in my quest to catch those beastly ghosts. Don't let me see you anywhere near it – or else!"

"No, boss!"

"You know whose this is, don't you, De-Sniff?"

De-Sniff thought hard.

"You don't reckon it belongs to that shoeshine boy, do you?"

Mrs Croker looked down at the brush as it lay before her.

"Oh yes, I think so. And now it's here, it gives me *power*, De-Sniff, *great power*. Now I will be able to follow those ghosts into their own world. I will be able to fly. I will be able to go anywhere I want. I will be invincible, De-Sniff. Invincible!"

Chapter 9

A Very Big Crush

"It's no use, Roddy," Tessa said. "I can't breathe. It's crushing the life out of us!"

Roddy and Tessa had been forced closer and closer together as the walls had moved in, making the room so small it was like being shut in a tiny box. There was no space left in it.

"Get me out!" Tessa screamed. "Please, somebody. Help!"

Roddy's chest felt as if it was being flattened. The walls of the room kept pushing and pushing, harder and harder, until Tessa had been shoved against Roddy and they were squeezed into each other. No matter how much they tried they couldn't get out. It was as if they'd fallen into a giant press – the sort that squashes the juice out of apples – and they would only be allowed out when they dribbled out as liquid.

Beads of sweat broke out on Tessa's forehead. Her teeth were jammed shut and her mouth was taut.

Suddenly something cold and small and misty was in there with them. It was something that whizzed round in front of them and then settled right on the tip of Roddy's nose.

"Hang on, mates!" cried a chirpy voice. It was William Povey, the ghost-boy, shrunk to the size of a pea. Roddy looked at him down his nose, going cross-eyed as he did so.

"Here, hold me hands!" William said.

His hands whizzed out from the sides of his tiny body on two arms which were as thin as a pair of skipping ropes.

Roddy and Tessa grabbed a hand each and at once became invisible. William then passed straight through the walls of the squeezing cell, taking Roddy and Tessa with him, out into the wide open space of the corridor.

"Oh," Tessa moaned, rubbing her shoulders and ribs. She took great gulps of air.

Roddy rubbed his chest. He shook his arms and legs to get them back into working order.

"What were you doing?" William chuckled as he grew back to normal size. "Trying to become the smallest people in the world, was yer?"

"Thank goodness you came!" Tessa said.

"Yeah," Roddy said, looking at his old friend. "Thanks, William."

"But what are you doing here?" Tessa said.

"What are *you* doing here, more like!" William answered.

"We got dragged here!" Roddy said and went on to tell William the whole story.

"So you thought it was me pulling the brushes?"

"Yes!" Tessa said.

"Well it weren't me, mate," William said. "In fact, *I* was yanked here meself, I was. Just like you."

William now explained how he'd gone to Tessa and Roddy's house to see if they could help him find Eric.

"Then all of a sudden, I was by the window. Something yanked me through it. And kept pulling me all the way here. I was just over the other side of the river when it stopped. Then I saw this place! Thought I'd come across and have a dekko. Then I found your bracelet, Tessa. Just on the shore. Good job I did!"

"You can say that again," Tessa said. She took the bracelet from him and put it on her arm.

"We thought you were here!" Roddy said.

As he spoke, the pale lights in the corridor began to flicker. This was followed by a horrible ghoulish noise, which screeched through the air.

"Let's get out," Tessa said. "I hate it! And we've got to get home, before morning."

"I can't leave yet," William whispered. "Not before I see what it was that was calling me. Anyway, this place ... I dunno why, but it seems familiar, you know. As if I been here before."

"It's *horrible*!" Tessa said. "You can't stay, William. Not on your own. Please don't!"

"No," Roddy said. "Look, William, we've *got* to get home. We've had a nightmare of a time. We're still wet through. Our parents will be worried to death if we're not there in the morning. And we simply can't get back without you!"

"Not without the brushes," Tessa said.

William stared at them for a moment.

"This house," he said. "It's bringing back memories. It's *so* peculiar."

"No kidding," Roddy cried. "Come on, William, take us home, please!"

"All right," William said. "But I've gotta come back."

Tessa didn't look very enthusiastic.

"You realize," William said anxiously, "that if those brushes fall into the wrong hands, it could be very dangerous for me?"

"Let's get back home and we can talk about it all tomorrow, eh?" Roddy said.

"Hold my hands again," William said.

As soon as they did so, they felt the cold shiver run along their tired and bruised limbs, right up through their bodies. Then they rose into the air, passed through the thick stone walls and flew off into the night. No force tried to heave them away from the direction they were taking – and it was so good to be going home.

Tessa and Roddy stared back at the snaking river far below, at the twinkling lights of the city, at the shape and curve of the land as it was laid out beneath them and, in the dim distance, at the hunched outline of the house from which they'd just escaped.

Back at home, Roddy and Tessa felt good to be warm and dry and safe again.

"Flying all the way back from London has nearly stopped my arm muscles working!" Roddy said, rubbing them to try and bring some life back into them.

"Mine are the same," Tessa said. "It's just such a long way to travel like that."

William, however, took no notice. He moped about the room. He was worrying. First he floated up to the top of the wardrobe. Then he shrank himself and lay down on the computer. Then he got up and whizzed round the room so fast, parts of him got left behind and only caught up with him when he came to rest, full size again, sitting next to Tessa on Roddy's bed.

"Calm down," Tessa whispered. "It won't help if you go into mega-dive of the spirits!"

William sighed.

"I been flying round and about looking for Eric, ever since I seen you last," he said. "And I ain't never even so much as caught sight of De-Sniff again!"

"And that's why you came back?" Roddy said.

"Yeah. And I was missing you an' all," William smiled. It was a really impish smile. "I was missing your computer as well. And your arguments and all the fun we had, especially at school!"

"We missed you," Tessa said.

Suddenly they heard a voice.

"Tessa? Is that you?"

Roddy's door opened.

"What are you doing?" Mr Oliver growled. He was bleary-eyed. His pyjamas were crumpled up. His hair was ruffled up in a grotesque heap, like a porcupine's back. "Do you realize it's four o'clock in the morning?"

Tessa got up quickly and hurried past him.

"Sorry Dad … I was just telling Roddy to stop snoring…"

"Huh!" Mr Oliver muttered. He turned round and bumped into the doorpost.

"You're sleepwalking, Dad," Roddy called.

Mr Oliver groaned grumpily and went back to bed.

Roddy slipped under the covers and turned off the light.

"I don't snore," he said. "Do I?"

"That's what you fink," William said.

Chapter 10

The Plan

"Wake up!" William shouted in Roddy's ear. "It's ten o'clock! You'll be late for school!"

Roddy groaned.

"School, Roddy!" William said again.

"There *isn't* any school today!" Roddy yelled. "It's the summer holidays, you great twit!"

"You don't have to go to school then?"

"Course not," Roddy said, turning over and slowly sitting up. He rubbed his eyes. "We've got at least six weeks off from the place!"

"Six weeks?" William said. "What? You mean you ain't got no school nor nothing to do for six whole weeks? Blimey!"

"This is civilized England, William," Roddy said. "We're not living in the Dark Ages!"

"Blimey!" William said again. "I never once had a couple of days off together from the shoeshine stall. Only day we didn't go down Picadilly was on Sunday and then we had to go to church."

"Glad I wasn't alive then," Roddy said as he got out of bed and got dressed.

"I've been thinking about the brushes," William said.

"Yeah, I know," Roddy said. "We'll have a talk in the den after breakfast, right?"

"Right," William said. "Can I have a go on the computer while you're eating?"

"Yes," Roddy said. "But don't go getting up to level eight! I'm still only on seven!"

"It'll take me mind off fings if I got a game to play, won't it?"

Roddy switched on the computer and went down for breakfast.

It was while they were eating that Mrs Oliver came into the room. She was as white as a sheet.

"Roddy!" she whispered. "There's something strange happening in your room!"

"Eh?" Roddy said, missing his mouth with the spoon and poking it into his cheek instead. Cereal spilled all down the side of his face.

"What d'you mean, Mum?"

"I just went in to collect your dirty washing…" Mrs Oliver whispered.

"Yeah?" Tessa said in a low voice.

"And … and the computer was on…"

"Yeah?" Tessa said again, thinking that her mother had somehow managed to see William.

Mrs Oliver stared at them in shock.

"The game was being played, all by itself as if … as if an invisible hand was working it!"

Tessa and Roddy gawped at each other.

"It's probably a spook, Mum," Roddy said, lightly. "You're always saying you want to see a spook, aren't you?"

Mrs Oliver grabbed the back of the chair to support herself. Her legs were trembling.

"Yes, I know, but … come and look!"

Tessa and Roddy rushed upstairs to Roddy's bedroom. Roddy gestured to William to stop.

"There's nothing here, Mum," Roddy called as she came in. He peered under the bed, pretending to search. William whooshed down there with him and sat amongst the old toys and dirty underpants.

"Mum's suspicious," Roddy hissed.

William gave a cheeky grin. The next moment,

he grabbed the pair of underpants and floated with them out from under the bed. The pants were covered in dust. William held them up, laughing.

"'Ere," he cried. "What's these things?"

Mrs Oliver saw the pants as they floated in front of her.

Roddy snatched them out of William's hands and clutched them in his hands.

"They ... they were floating..." Mrs Oliver gasped. Her eyes showed she was horrified.

"No, Mum," Tessa said. "They're disgusting enough to be able to move by themselves, but they weren't really. It was just Roddy's little trick, wasn't it, Roddy?"

"Er ... oh, yes," he said. "Bit of cotton, Mum."

"Bit of cotton?" Mrs Oliver said.

"Roddy pulling on it," Tessa said. "Old trick."

"What is going on?" Mrs Oliver said, more firmly now.

"Nothing, Mum." Roddy glared at William.

Mrs Oliver looked again at the computer. The game was waiting for somebody to play it.

"It's been on since I got up," Roddy said.

"I tell you somebody was using it!" Mrs Oliver snapped. "I'm not incapable of knowing what I saw!"

"Trick of the mind?" Tessa suggested.

"It was *not* a trick of the mind!" Mrs Oliver shouted. "I distinctly saw the keys move and figures shooting each other on the screen!" She turned round to them. "And don't look at me like that! As if I'm going potty!"

Just as she was leaving, a score came up on the computer screen, showing that somebody *must have been* playing on it very recently.

Mrs Oliver shivered involuntarily and rushed out of the room.

William giggled and floated up to the ceiling.

"You idiot!" Roddy said. "You're succeeding in scaring Mum daft! She thinks the house is haunted!"

"Well, it is!" William cried.

"Don't do any more tricks," Tessa said. "It's not fair!"

"All right," William sighed. "Sorry, mates. I reckon I been getting so tense lately, I needed a bit of fun to cheer me up!"

"Don't worry about it," Tessa said. "Mum'll forget about it in a couple of days."

"But I thought she liked spooks," William said.

"Yeah, she says she does," Roddy replied. "As long as they're elsewhere, I guess."

Later that morning, after breakfast, Roddy and Tessa and William went out to their den — a crumbling old brick outhouse their father had said they could use. It was covered in ivy and had pigeons living in it, not to mention bats in its roof.

"I've *got* to go back to that old mansion!" William said. "And the sooner the better."

"We ought to come with you," Roddy said. "It's not right that you should go alone."

"Yeah? Well, I'd like you both to come wiv me," William said.

"I *hate* that house," Tessa said. "But I don't want *you* to go in there and face it by yourself."

"If we could think of a plan so that we can go to London and stay there for a while," Roddy said, "it would be easier. We wouldn't have to keep worrying about getting home."

"But how?" Tessa cried. "Mum and Dad won't let us, even if we want to."

"No," William said. "I'll just have to go by meself. I can't wait around. Look, I'm really sorry. I probably shouldn't have come back here, bothering you, like. And I do really appreciate what you're trying to do. But I ain't got time to wait around. I really ain't. I have to get them brushes. That's vital. And another thing. I been thinkin' – what if old sniffy nose is something to do with all this? The brushes being called and that?"

"You think it's possible?" Tessa cried.

"Oh yeah," William said. "The Ghost Hunter may be dead, but De-Sniff is still very much alive and kicking. "

"I think we *should* come with you," Roddy said. "And if De-Sniff is anything at all to do with the brushes, it makes it even more important. Give us a bit of time."

"Come on," Tessa said, "let's go and have a stroll round the village and see what's going on. It might help us to work out a plan as well."

"Yeah, all right," William said. "But can you bring a jar wiv you? I don't feel that happy since I got yanked halfway across the country yesterday. So I been finking, if that power or whatever it was comes back, there ain't nuffink I can do, see. But if you popped me in a jar, it might not get me."

"Right," Tessa said. "There's one over here." She reached behind her and from a table with three legs – the other leg had been replaced by a pile of bricks – she picked up a jar. "This should do."

Then they climbed down the rickety stairs of

the outhouse and ambled down the garden. As they did so, Mrs Oliver rushed out of the back kitchen door. She was still pale – paler, if anything.

"Roddy, Tessa," she said. "There's a ghost in the house, I'm sure of it! A plate just fell off the table and broke!"

"No, Mum," Tessa said, "you probably nudged it or something as you walked past."

"But I wasn't anywhere near it!" she cried. "And another thing, a letter came this morning from Aunty Marion – inviting us to stay with her? Well that got torn up all by itself. You didn't do it, did you?"

The children shook their heads. Mrs Oliver went back into the house.

"She's really spooked!" Tessa shouted. "You've got to stop doing this sort of thing, William!"

"Me?" William cried innocently. "I didn't do nuffink!"

"Oh yes, you did!" Tessa cried.

"I tell you I didn't!" William shouted back hotly.

"Well, if you didn't," Tessa said, suspiciously, "who did?"

Chapter 11

The Dark Shadow

As they were going past Mrs Gardener's stables, Wally Crabbe sneered at them.

"Where you two twits going then?" he said.

"There and back to see how far it is," Roddy replied.

"Oh yeah? Clever drip ain't you, Oliver?"

"If I'm a drip, you must be a pond," Roddy said quickly. "A stagnant one!"

"Who you calling stagnant?" Wally shouted.

"I'm not *calling* you it, I'm smelling you," Roddy said.

"Now don't start," Tessa said soothingly. "What are you doing here, anyway, Wally?"

"Cleaning out Ma Gardener's stables, ain't I?"

"What for?" Tessa said.

"Money! That's what for!" Wally cried. "Spending money for when I go on holiday with Uncle Jake."

"You're going on holiday with Old Nosey – I mean your uncle?" Roddy gasped.

"Yeah. So? What if I am? He's my favourite uncle! And I don't mind a bit of mucky work if it gets me plenty of dosh. In fact I quite like muck." Wally scraped a bit of horse manure off his boot and flicked it at Roddy. " 'Ere, try some."

"Hey, stop that!" Roddy shouted.

Wally laughed loudly.

"Good for you, a bit of muck is, eh Oliver? Put some in yer shoes – might make you grow a bit!"

"Hey," William shouted in Roddy's ear. "Don't let him get away wiv that! Give him one on the nose!"

Roddy shook his head.

"All right, if you won't do somefink, I will!" William cried.

"No!" Tessa yelled. But William took no notice. Tessa grabbed Roddy's arm and tried to lead him away.

"Yeah, go on," Wally Crabbe shouted, "go and run down the street and play Barbies with your sister!"

"I beg your pardon!" Tessa shouted angrily.

"I bet you still play with *dolls*, don't you?" Wally shouted. "I bet you got a little Sindy or a little Baby Jane somewhere, ain't you?"

"No, I have not!" Tessa shouted. "And even if I *did* want to play with dolls, what's it got to do with you?"

A nice row was brewing now and Wally was loving it. He was sniggering from ear to ear.

"I bet when no one's looking you get your doll's pram out and push them dollies about in it, don't you?"

"You're a stupid fool!" Tessa cried hotly.

"No, it ain't me that's stupid," Wally laughed, "it's you! Nearly fourteen and still playing with dolls! Ha! I bet you say things like, 'Come on then ickle darling, come to mummy,' don't you? Eh?"

"No, I do not!" Tessa shouted. "And what if I did? I bet you spend your time playing soldiers, don't you?"

Suddenly, from Mrs Gardener's yard, a contraption rolled up behind Wally. It was an old pram that had been left out in the farmyard for years. It had four wheels and a handle to push it with and it had a hood, which at this moment was pushed down. The inside of the thing was steaming slightly and gave off a strong smell. But Wally Crabbe didn't notice at all. He was much too busy calling Tessa names.

"You're a nappy freak, you are!" he mocked. "Off your trolley! Or should I say, off your pram! Ha! Ha!"

Suddenly, William, who Wally couldn't see, shoved the pram into the back of Wally's knees.

"Oi, what the…?" Wally yelled. He stumbled backwards and fell right into the old pram, which William had brought up behind him.

"Oi! What's going on?" Wally screeched again as he flopped back and then floundered about in the pram. The pram began to be wheeled about.

Roddy and Tessa hooted with laughter, for Wally Crabbe was lying back in a pram full of chicken droppings.

"It's you that plays with prams!" Tessa laughed. "Bye–bye, smelly ickle dumpling."

"Eh!" Wally yelled. Then, as he tried to scramble out of the pram, he put his hands behind him and they sank right up to the wrists in the mess.

"You done this!" he shouted down the street after them. He stood waving his smelly fist in the air while the backside of his trousers steamed as if he was on fire. "I'll get you lot for this!" he shrieked. "I'll get you!"

Tessa and Roddy and William hurried away down the lane. Behind them, Wally Crabbe carried on bellowing like an angry bull.

"That was *brilliant*, William!" Tessa said.

"But dangerous," Roddy said. "Drawing attention to yourself like that."

"He didn't know nuffink," William said with a chuckle. "And anyway, the Ghost Hunter's a goner, ain't she? So there's nobody here to worry about."

They walked through the village until they were outside the shop. Suddenly, Tessa's friend Catherine called to her.

"Hey, Tess! Hey come here a minute!"

Tessa crossed the road to Catherine's house and stood chatting. Roddy and William waited, drooling over the sweets in the shop window. As they looked in, Roddy saw a shadow pass across the glass – a dark shadow. He looked at William, but William hadn't noticed.

A dark shadow! Roddy's skin crawled along his back as the shadow vanished into thin air. Roddy immediately thought of the Ghost Hunter. But she was dead, wasn't she? Then he thought of the great gloomy mansion they'd been in the previous night. Something odd was happening again. He could sense it.

"Hey, look what Catherine's given me!" Tessa called as she ran back to join them. She was waving a magazine.

"What is it?" Roddy said.

"Spooky News!" Tessa said. "It's a psychic mag. For Mum!"

Roddy leaned over Tessa's shoulder and looked at the magazine. He began to read. After a few moments he shouted, "This is just what we need!"

"Pardon?" Tessa said, wrinkling up her nose. "Need for what?"

"For my plan, of course. I've just thought of a good one. And it will solve our biggest problem..."

Chapter 12

Holiday Where?

Tessa hurried into the house, still holding the magazine, followed by Roddy and William.

"Mum!" Tessa called at the top of her voice. "Mum!"

Mrs Oliver came out of her office. "What on earth's the matter?" she said.

"We just wanted to show you this advert!"

Mrs Oliver read out loud, "Psychic Research Conference." Then she read all the smaller detailed print to herself.

"A conference in London?" she said. "Studying ghosts and other paranormal happenings? That would be wonderful!"

"We could stay with Aunty Marion," Roddy said quickly. "She lives in London."

"Yeah, Mum," Tessa cried, "it would be great!

We could enjoy ourselves seeing all the sights while you're at the course."

"I don't want to go away at the moment, not with all the pyschic activity going on *here*. It's scary, but I want to investigate it properly. Anyway, I thought you wanted to go to Wales again."

"No!" Roddy said. "Let's go to London instead!"

"Not while there are spooks about," Mrs Oliver said.

Roddy groaned and looked at William.

"See!" he muttered.

"It ain't my fault!" William huffed.

"Well, if you hadn't…"

Mrs Oliver was staring at Roddy.

"Who are you talking to?" she said.

"Oh…er…nobody. Just, er, just thinking aloud, Mum!"

Mrs Oliver went off shaking her head, with the magazine under her arm.

Roddy, Tessa and William went out to the den and sat around looking glum.

"It was a good idea," Tessa said.

"Yeah, nice try," William sighed. "It looks as if I gotta go back on me own," he said firmly.

"Give me a bit more time!" Roddy cried. "I've only just mentioned it to her. And for heaven's sake, don't go doing any more things which she might think are spooky!"

"But I don't always fink, do I? Tell you what. I'll give yer till this evening to persuade 'em and if not, I'm off to see if Eric's at that house!"

Tessa looked desperately at Roddy.

"All right," she said.

But then something unexpected upset everything. Including William.

It was later that day. The whole family sat down to their evening meal. Mr Oliver had come home early after putting the main roof timbers up on a new house in the village. He was tired. Mrs Oliver had flopped down in her seat, tired out as well after cooking the meal, washing and working on her computer for several hours. Roddy and Tessa sat in their usual places. William had stayed in the bedroom playing on Roddy's computer.

"It's only lasagne," Mrs Oliver said.

"I love lasagne," Tessa said.

"I don't know what on earth you two have been

doing with your clothes," Mrs Oliver said, "but they stank. They were absolutely filthy!"

Tessa looked across at Roddy, remembering their trip into the disgusting cellar.

"Sorry, Mum," she said.

"Just take a bit more care," Mrs Oliver said. "And Roddy, one of your trainers is absolutely soaking and I can't see the other one anywhere? What have you been doing?"

"Er... nothing, Mum," Roddy said.

"I expect a crocodile ate it," Tessa giggled. Roddy glared at her.

Mr Oliver had picked up the evening paper and was glancing at the headlines before he began eating.

Suddenly the paper was smacked out of his hands and was frenziedly torn into pieces. Roddy and Tessa gasped as they saw a dark shadow zip across the room and vanish through the wall. Mr and Mrs Oliver, of course, couldn't see the shadow at all.

Mr Oliver, completely taken by surprise, stared first at Roddy and Tessa and then at Mrs Oliver.

Mrs Oliver was staring at him, her mouth wide open with shock.

A second later, the dark shadow whizzed back through the wall, seized Mr Oliver's lasagne from right in front of him and tipped it over his head. The tablecloth was suddenly snatched from the table and all the dishes and cutlery went flying across the room.

"Aarghhh!" Mrs Oliver screamed as she dived for cover.

Roddy jumped to his feet. He bolted out of the room and ran to the bedroom. Tessa followed.

"William!" Roddy howled as he threw open the door.

"What's up mate?"

"You!" Roddy shouted.

But before he could say another word, William was knocked backwards through the computer screen and then through the wall. Roddy heard a terrible scream as William came hurtling back into the bedroom, with the shadowy figure tearing at him and fighting him for all he was worth.

Right in front of his eyes, Roddy witnessed a fantastic battle. It was like two cats clawing and tearing at each other. Bits of William floated off and then came back – first his ear, then some of his arm, then his nose. Bits of black were torn off the shadow and went drifting away, only to return a few moments later. The noises – screaming, shouting, growling – were awful.

Roddy saw William raise his fist and whack the black shadow so hard it whizzed across the room and splattered through the wardrobe.

All went quiet. After a few moments, William said, "I fink it's gone."

"But what was it?" Roddy asked in a hushed, terrified whisper.

"It was what's known as a Tear-Away Shadow," William said.

"What's that?" Tessa hissed.

"It's a ghost," William said. "But a very angry young ghost that won't do what it's told, and goes berserk at the slightest thing."

"Phew!" Roddy said. "Well, d'you think that's the last we'll see of it?"

"Dunno," William said.

"What brought it here?" Tessa squeaked.

"Probably just an accident," William said. "It probably didn't expect to find another ghost here, either."

"You know, William," Roddy said. "I saw

something strange in the shop window this afternoon – a sort of black shadow."

"That was it," William said, "most likely."

Tessa flopped down on the bed.

"That was scary!" she murmured.

Mr Oliver poked his head round the door.

"Roddy?" he said. "Are you all right?"

"Yes. Are you?"

"I am now, but your mother's going crazy with all these strange goings on."

"You don't think it could all have been ... a ... well ... an accident?" Roddy said.

"What? The plate flying up like that? The tablecloth pulled from the table? No, there was definitely something – I've heard of polter-geists."

"Dad," Roddy said. "Why don't you try and get Mum to agree to go to London for a holiday? Aunty Marion's invited us and Mum could go on that Psychic Awareness course and it would get us all away from the house."

"Good idea," Mr Oliver said. "Your mum's been overworking. It might even be the cause of this ... this ... *activity*, whatever it is. You know, force fields and electric energy et cetera?"

"Yes," Roddy agreed enthusiastically. "That's probably all it is, Dad."

A smile came to Mr Oliver's face.

"Well done," he said as he walked out of the room. "I'll go and put it to your mother this minute, if she's in a fit state yet to listen!"

The next day, when Roddy, Tessa and William were in the village, Mrs Oliver had been working at her new article on "Ghosts of Little Henlock", when the kitchen tap suddenly started running. She heard it at once as it was pumping water out into the bowl at full force. She rushed into the kitchen and turned it off. As soon as she did so, a saucepan fell on to the floor making a terrible clatter.

"Oh no!" Mrs Oliver cried. "Not again."

As she bent down to pick the saucepan up, a bag of flour emptied over her head. This was too much for Mrs Oliver. She screamed and ran out of the house. It was at that moment that Roddy, Tessa and William came back.

"What's happened, Mum?" Tessa asked, when she saw her mum's frightened face, dabbed with flour, and her hair all white.

"I … I've just had that spook back again," her

mother cried. "It's turning on taps, throwing saucepans and … and emptying flour over me!"

"Wait here," Roddy said. "Tessa, come with me."

They entered the kitchen, with William right beside them.

"We've got to sort this out," Roddy said.

As he spoke, a dark shadow whisked past his face and flew up the stairs. William darted after it.

"Wait," Roddy cried.

But William had gone. Tessa stared round the kitchen. It was like a bomb site.

"Come on," Roddy said. "William might need help!"

They ran upstairs as fast as they could and flung open the bedroom door, just in time to see the mad shadow as it tore out through the top of a wardrobe and zipped across the room, howling and shrieking like a whirlwind. Round and round the room it flew, with William after it. Then William and the shadow began to fight again. Through the ceiling, through the floor, through the walls they thwacked each other. And every time they came back fighting and spitting. Suddenly there wasn't just the shadow and William, there was a cat in there as well. It was slashing with its paws and spitting and biting for all its worth.

"Stop!" Roddy yelled. But they didn't listen. They just carried on smashing their fists into each other. And the cat went on wailing like a banshee. Whoever or whatever the shadow was, it was unstoppable. At least it looked unstoppable. And now the cat had got on to William's head and was clawing at his scalp.

Roddy couldn't think how to help his friend before he was torn to shreds. But as the battle raged about him, he saw something which stunned him. The black shadow fighting like a panther was a girl! Before he had time to exclaim though, something else happened. Something even more incredible.

William plunged his hand right into the shadow, and held on in such a way that she couldn't get away. Almost at once, she collapsed and floated like a rag doll in front of him. The cat vanished.

"It's all right, mate," William panted. "It's a Tear-Away Shadow. But I got her *inner heart* right here."

"Inner heart?" Roddy mumbled.

"Yeah, all ghosts have 'em," William said, "but you have to know just how to hold 'em."

"Let go of me!" the shadow spat at William. "Just you let go!"

"What you doing here?" William said, his body, wobbling and trembling after the fight.

"What's it gotta do with you? Let me GO!" The shadow wriggled and twisted, but she couldn't get free.

"It's got everything to do wiv me," William cried. "Especially after you nearly knocked me block off! And especially after you been breaking this house into bits and scaring the living daylights out of Mrs Oliver!"

The shadow went still. And as she did so, her face appeared in sharper focus and the darkness went out of her form.

"All right," she said.

"Eh, hang on a minute," William said. "You're unhappy, ain't you?"

"Get lost!" the girl cried. "Let me go!" She stared angrily at William and then began to struggle. When she found she still couldn't get free, she stopped fighting again.

"Where you from?" William said.

"London – if it's got anything to do with you! I've had a horrible time!" she snapped. "Who are you?"

"William Povey," William said. "Ghost since Queen Victoria's time."

He suddenly let go of the Tear-Away Shadow.

"Who are you?"

Now the Tear-Away Shadow looked hard at William.

"Flora."

They stood looking at each other. "What happened to you?" Flora asked.

"What happened?" William replied. "I got run over, I did."

Flora said. "I got put in an orphanage when I was little and died along with loads of other kids. I was all right till then!"

"How did yer die?" William said.

"Wasn't just me," Flora said. "It was everybody in there, including the superintendent, Mr Breakham. Nasty bloke he is an' all. There was an almighty fire!"

"And?" William said.

"I just didn't want to die," Flora said. "I just wouldn't. Nor would any of 'em, including Breakham. And when we became ghosts, Breakham wouldn't let us free! He cut off any way of escape wiv Ectofirm. He forced us to stay. So we were stuck; trapped in that dismal hole! Except I just got out, didn't I? After all this time! Load of other orphans still in there. I wanna get them out. They're all good kids, they are, and they're just stuck in that place with that horrible Breakham. I just been getting angrier and angrier wiv people. And that's when I went berserk in here. Sorry."

"Wait a minute," William said. "Meet my two pals. Two really good mates. Tessa and Roddy. Saved my bacon they have, a couple of times."

"Pleased to meet you," Flora said cautiously. "Here, how come they can see me?"

"Second sight, gel," William said. "Brilliant it is!"

"I saw you yesterday, at the shop," Flora said.

"Yes," Roddy replied. "I saw you too – or at least, I saw a black shadow. That was you?"

"Yeah, that was me. When I'm really angry, I get a black shadow on me," Flora said. "It was me here, before and all. Upsetting the woman – is she your mother?"

"Yes!" Roddy said. "So it was you who broke the plate and ripped up the letter?"

"I was so angry! That's why I am here!"

"Angry with what?" William cried.

"With dying, with that orphanage, with

Breakham! With people who won't see me! Even with normal ghosts!"

"With me?" William said.

"You ain't *normal*, William!" she murmured.

A pair of beautiful, dark ghostly eyes now lifted themselves up and flickered at Roddy for a moment.

"I ain't got nowhere to go," she murmured.

"Well, you can't stay here," Roddy said. "You've already caused enough havoc. My parents are going round the twist, thanks to you."

"Let me stay," she said. "Just till I work out how to get my mates free of the orphanage. Please! I won't do no harm any more."

"We don't know that," William said. "You might go berserk again as soon as the mood gets on yer."

"I won't. I promise. I can behave sometimes. When I am treated well. I was just at the end of my wits. What with thinking about all them mates of mine trapped in that horrible place and me not knowing what to do."

"You got to behave all the time, gel, whatever!" William cried. "You can't go around acting like a mad poltergeist!"

"If you let me stay for a while, I will be good."

Flora said. "And maybe you could come and help me, Will, to save my friends?" she said, putting her head on one side.

"What d'you think, Roddy?" William said.

At that moment there was a shrill sound which emanated from Flora's pocket. Roddy and William looked at her for an explanation. Flora smiled and reached down. As her hand came to rest, a head popped up under it. It was the head of a very weird cat.

"This is Nooby," she said softly. "My spectral cat."

The cat they had seen earlier, fighting like a tiger, now emerged from her pocket and stretched upwards gripping her sleeve. In one swift movement, it darted up her arm and stood alarmingly on her shoulder. It was alarming because it had huge almond-shaped eyes, which flashed like fire, and two bitten and battered ears, one larger than the other. He had a wagging, angry tail and he put out his claws as if to show how many he'd got.

"It's all right, Nooby," Flora said. "These are my *new* friends."

The cat turned its head away indifferently.

"He's a fighter," Flora said.

Tessa stared at Flora who was sitting on Roddy's bed, stroking the strange cat.

Flora turned and gave Tessa a long, shrewd penetrating look.

"Can I stay, then?" she said.

Tessa shivered slightly.

"I guess so. If William's happy about it. But no more shenanigans!" Tessa said. "No more breakages! No more terrifying my poor mum!"

Chapter 13

Spirits of Eternity

De-Sniff looked longingly at the brush as it lay in its brand new glass case on the bench, next to Mrs Croker. She took it everywhere with her now, and De-Sniff was not allowed to pass within a couple of metres of it without her glaring accusingly at him. She was different now ... different from how she was before she fell from the castle ramparts.

"Hey, boss," De-Sniff said, "you know when you fell in that moat?"

"What about it?" the Ghost Hunter snapped.

"Well how *did* you get out?"

Mrs Croker sneered.

"My great-grandfather, De-Sniff," she said. "Obadiah Quirke."

"Your great-grandfather? That bloke in that painting? But he's … he's dead, ain't he, boss?"

"Oh yes, he's dead. But when I was struggling in the water, fighting for my life in those strangling weeds, I saw his face. As clear as I see yours."

"Weird," De-Sniff muttered.

"And then I knew I couldn't give up my quest. I had to fulfil my destiny!"

De-Sniff stared at Mrs Croker as if she was completely bats.

"Oh," he said. "What destiny's that then, boss?"

She turned away from him and went on repairing the Spectrika, which was on the bench before her.

"To undo all that ruined him when he was alive. To restore the fortunes of my family! To take revenge!"

"Oh," De-Sniff nodded.

"A few more nuts and bolts," she mumbled, "and it'll be back to its old self."

"You done a good job on that, boss," De-Sniff said.

"Oh yes. I've done a *very* good job! Except that I can't get the antenna to work any more, thanks to you!" Mrs Croker snarled. "It's a good thing the rest of it wasn't completely pulverized!"

"Sorry, boss," De-Sniff said. "Still, no harm done."

"No harm done!" Mrs Croker puffed. "But when it's completely back together, I shall need ghosts, De-Sniff."

"You got some already, boss. You got that old Eric and you got a few others what you already had in your collection."

"I need more than them. I need ninety-nine in total." She glanced at the calculations on her bench. She ran her finger along them.

"Yes. Ninety-nine ghosts will create enough energy for my purposes. If I've done my calculations right."

"Calculations?" De-Sniff said as he picked up a stuffed toad and waggled it about in the air. "What you calculating then, boss? How rich you're gonna be?"

"No, De-Sniff," Mrs Croker said. "Although I do intend to be rich! But I am after something even more exciting and permanent than money!"

"What's that then?" he said. "I can't see what ninety-nine ghosts can do for you. What d'you want 'em for, boss?"

"To put in the Spectrika. That's what for."

"What? In that globe thing? Keep 'em all in there?"

"Yes," Mrs Croker said.

"But how will that help?" He tried to go nearer to peer over her shoulder at the figures she kept referring to.

"Stay back!" she snapped. "This has to be a perfectly clean operation. No stray nose-pickings in the machinery, thank you very much."

De-Sniff nervously wiped his conk down his sleeve and coughed.

"But what's it all do, boss?" he asked again as he took a step backwards.

"I've already told you! Ninety-nine ghosts will deliver enough spectral energy…"

"For what, though?" De-Sniff persisted.

"To create the conditions to give me the power to travel through time!" Mrs Croker hissed. She turned round to face him now, and her eyes glowed.

"Through time?" De-Sniff whispered and took a step back.

"Yes," she said. "When I nearly died in that moat, after you had deserted me, I was given new power, De-Sniff. And part of that power is to devise the means to do this!"

"So that thing, that Specko, is the means?"

"Yes. All I have to do is fill it with ninety-nine ghosts, sit in this special seat and then press this button here, and kapatz! The energy will start a chain reaction in the Spectrika."

De-Sniff was staring at her.

"So you mean, boss," De-Sniff repeated with growing awe, "that you can then travel through to *any* time?"

"Yes. So I shall *never* have to experience the *horror* of becoming a ghost myself. I shall be able to move forwards and backwards. For ever!"

"Barmy as a bat," De-Sniff muttered, as he saw her eyes.

"What did you say?" Mrs Croker screamed.

"Nothing, boss. I was just thinking that anyone else would think that it was barmy, but I know it ain't."

"It's what Man has longed to do, De-Sniff. Ever since the Egyptians created the means to embalm their dead. To live on, passing through time. I am at the forefront of what will be commonplace in two hundred years' time."

"What? You mean everybody's gonna do it?"

"Eventually, yes."

De-Sniff glanced at the Spectrika, then at the newly constructed Energy Chair, then at her.

"And the ghosts, they give the power?" he said.

"Yes. They have special energy, which can be compressed. And, by directing that energy properly, the boundaries which separate worlds can be dissolved!"

"Wowee," De-Sniff said softly, though he didn't really understand what she was talking about. "That's impressive, boss."

"So we need ghosts. And especially young ghosts."

"Young uns?"

"Because they've got more power than any others."

"Can I come with you, when you become a Time Flipper?" De-Sniff asked.

"No. There is room only for one. And that one is Me!" Mrs Croker said.

"Oh," De-Sniff said, sadly. "I want to go as well."

"Tough," Mrs Croker said. "But I'll still be around. I shall come back, and leave again, and never die."

Mrs Croker now crossed the room to a safe and

unlocked it. She took from it the jar containing Eric.

"I think we'll blow this one in to the Spectrika and then we'll go out. I haven't been out for a long time."

Eric looked terrified. He stood up and was waving about, wanting to be let free. But Mrs Croker took no notice and when De-Sniff saw him he began laughing and pulling faces at him.

"I don't like that one," De-Sniff said. "He tried to punch me at Chillwood Castle."

The Ghost Hunter ignored her assistant. She simply fastened the jar to the end of a nozzle, which in turn connected to the Spectrika.

After flicking a couple of switches and making sure the power system was on, Mrs Croker pressed the **Suck** button on the Spectrika. At once there was a high-pitched sound as a motor kicked into life and then the ghost was pulled, as if by a mighty wind, out of the jar and into the glass globe. For a few seconds he spun round and round, head over heels until he finally came to rest. Eric staggered about inside, looking sick and dizzy.

"I still have some fine adjustments to make," she told De-Sniff, "before the Spectrika is completely ready to go. And it won't work until the Ghostometer reads "full". So don't you go anywhere near it, do you understand?"

"Yes, boss," De-Sniff said. "You can rely on me." And he immediately went right up to the globe and started watching Eric.

"I said, *don't get too near it*!" Mrs Croker shouted. "Do I have to write it on your skull?"

De-Sniff jumped back quickly.

"No, boss. Sorry, boss. I forgot, boss!"

"Well, don't!" Mrs Croker said. "Just don't!"

"No, boss," De-Sniff said again, and glanced quietly at the Ghostometer reading. A glass tube, full of mercury, like a thermometer, showed that the Ghostometer now held one ghost.

At that moment, Horace entered the room after giving the door a discreet knock.

"Supper is ready, ma'am," he said. "And I've put Mr De-Sniff's in the servants' quarters."

"Servants?" De-Sniff growled.

"Yes, sir," Horace said.

De-Sniff eyed Horace maliciously, but Mrs Croker said, "You'd better bring it in here, Horace. I intend to go out immediately afterwards and I shan't be wanting to send out a search party!"

"Very well, ma'am," Horace replied, a little flickering smile playing round his lips. "I hope the meal will be satisfactory." He withdrew, then returned carrying two plates with lids over them. He set them down on the bench.

"This one is Mr De-Sniff's," he said.

"Oh good!" De-Sniff called, sitting down. Horace immediately left the room. Mrs Croker put down the tools she'd been holding and joined her apprentice.

"I could eat anything, I could!" De-Sniff cried. "My belly thinks me throat's cut." He lifted the lid from his meal and his mouth dropped open. On his plate was a piece of toast. And on the toast was a dead fly. And next to the dead fly was a live slug.

De-Sniff stared at them. Then he looked at Mrs Croker's meal. It was a beautiful, steaming curry.

"Come along," Mrs Croker said. "Eat up. We haven't got much time!"

De-Sniff had turned green. He flicked the fly away and poked the slug off the toast with a pencil. He lifted the toast up and examined it. There were signs that it had been around for a long time. A patch of mould was growing out of a corner. There were little rolled-up things too, which looked like mouse droppings. De-Sniff flicked them off. He wiped the toast on his sleeve. He turned it round and round. He sniffed at it.

"What are you playing at, man?" Mrs Croker snapped, as she ladled into her mouth a delicious forkful of rice. De-Sniff wrinkled his nose. Then he closed his eyes and bit into the toast.

Mrs Croker finished quickly. She then lifted up the case with the brush in it and looked at De-Sniff.

"That was delicious. Hurry up! We're going out."

"Out?" De-Sniff replied slowly. His stomach was bubbling and burbling. "I think I'm gonna be sick, boss," he said.

"You can't be sick!" Mrs Croker cried. "We haven't got time for that!"

She snatched him to his feet and cuffed his ears. Strangely, it made De-Sniff feel better.

"Where we going, boss?"

"We're going hunting, De-Sniff. Hunting for ghosts! I've got the Ghost Compass and I've got a powerful reading on a place where there's lots of young energy. We're going there!"

Chapter 14

Holiday in London

"Well, my darlings," Aunty Marion said, after she had greeted them all in the hallway, relieved them of their cases and taken them into the lovely old-fashioned sitting-room. "It's so *wonderful* to see you all. I expect you're all tired after that *awful* motorway, so I've made some chocolate cakes and things. Just sit down and put your feet up, will you?"

"I'm *so* glad we came!" Mr Oliver said. "It'll do us the world of good, won't it Jan?"

"Yes! I'm sure it will," Mrs Oliver replied, looking round the room. "Isn't this a gorgeous room? Roddy, don't touch!"

"Oh, I don't mind," Aunty Marion said, as she came back in, "touch anything you like, darling, it's all a load of old tat."

Roddy smiled.

"She's all right, your old aunt, ain't she?" William said, settling down on a heap of papers stacked up on the dresser.

"Come on, Roddy!" Mr Oliver called. "Cakes!"

Roddy and Tessa tucked in to the delicious cream and chocolate cakes. There was plenty of ice-cream and lemonade as well.

"Cor, wish I could eat that stuff!" William said, licking his lips. "I ain't never had ice-cream in me life!" He dipped his tongue into it. Roddy laughed. Mr Oliver looked at him sharply.

"What's the matter, Roddy?" he said.

"Nothing, Dad," Roddy said.

"Now what I want you to do," Aunty Marion said comfortably, "is to make this place your home for a couple of weeks. Your course will be easy to get to, Jan, and there are loads of museums and things for you, Colin, if you're interested. But do *please yourselves*!"

"We can look after ourselves, Dad," Tessa piped up. "No need for you to worry about us."

"Yeah," Roddy said. "We've got our own plans, haven't we, Tess?"

"Oh?" Mr Oliver said cheerfully. "That's fine, then."

Later on, Roddy and Tessa's aunt led them upstairs to the top floor – there were three altogether – and showed them into two small but pleasant rooms with views right over the river.

"It's beautiful!" Tessa cried. "A beautiful house!"

As soon as her aunt left, Tessa went into Roddy's room. William was there as well. Flora crawled slowly out of a suitcase by passing through its side.

"Comfy sleeping on your socks, Roddy," she said.

"Good job they were clean," Tessa said. "You'd never have slept on them if he'd just taken them off."

"Nice place, ain't it?" Flora said, looking round the room at the oak beams and the little lopsided windows.

"Cool, isn't it?" Tessa said.

"No, it ain't *cool* at all," Flora said. "It's warm!"

"And posh as well," William said. "Ain't it?"

"Near the river too," Roddy said. "Thank heavens we persuaded Mum to come down to that psycho course!"

"*Psychic*!" Tessa corrected. "We can do exactly what we want here, if we play our cards right, can't we?"

"Yeah," Roddy said. "Whatever happens, we mustn't let Dad drag us off on long 'interesting' expeditions!"

"We've got to get William's brushes back as soon as we can!" Roddy said.

"Let's go out and have a look round now," Tessa said. "We've just about got time and we're close to the river. Maybe we can spot the island?"

"What about my mates?" Flora cried. "I thought we could go and rescue them first!"

"We promised William we'd help him first," Roddy said.

"Yeah," William cried. "Let's go right now!"

"I'll just pop down and tell Mum and Dad," Tessa said. "Meet me in the street, OK?"

"I think we should go and get my mates!" Flora cried crossly. "You said you'd try and help me, Will! They need me! They need help NOW!!"

"All right, keep yer hair on!" William said gently.

"We will try and help you," Roddy said. "But you'll have to be patient. Your friends will be all right for a day or two, won't they?"

"No, they flippin' won't!" Flora yelled. "You don't know Breakham! You don't know what it's like!"

"We can't do everything at once!" Tessa said, trying to calm Flora down. "Be patient!"

"No, I won't!" Flora screeched. "I've been patient!" She got so angry that she vanished through the wall.

"She's just got the huff!" William said. "Take no notice. She'll be back."

"You don't think she'll start her old tricks, do you?" Tessa asked anxiously.

"Nah," William said. "I reckon she'll be here when we get back. She's just got a big chip on her shoulder, that's all."

Outside in the busy London street, Roddy glanced across the road at the great river, then he turned and looked down the road at the buildings. There were lots of offices and a few hotels. The nearest hotel to Aunty Marion's house was called The Mermaid Hotel.

"It's all changed," William sighed. "There weren't hardly any of this lot here in my time, mate. "It's gone mad, it has! Where's all the 'orses and carts and carriages? Eh?"

Tessa closed the solid front door of 7 Ravenbell Road.

"It's *so different*!" William said, his head whizzing left and right and sometimes all the way round as well.

They started to walk along the pavement, past the hotel, when a boy shot out of its front door, not looking where he was going, and banged right into Roddy, knocking him over.

"Ouch!" Roddy shouted.

"Watch where yer going!" the boy yelled. Then he stopped and stared at Roddy. Roddy got up off the pavement and stared at him.

" 'Ere, Oliver! What you doin' here?"

It was Wally Crabbe.

"Wally?" Roddy gasped.

"Don't say, sorry, will you?" Tessa said.

"He should look where he's going!" Wally said. "Gor … come down here for a bit of peace and holiday, we did. And look what turns up!"

"Holiday?" Tessa screeched.

"Yeah. Holiday! I told you I was saving up, didn't I. And what you doing down here?"

At that moment another familiar voice rang out across the pavement.

"Oi, you!"

Roddy and Tessa looked up sharply.

"Oh no," William said. "It's that Old Nosey geezer from that school what you go to. He's here an' all!"

Mr Harding came striding up to them. He looked slightly astonished.

"Can't get away from you, can we, Oliver? Eh? What you doing down here?"

As if Old Nosey wasn't enough, he was soon followed out of the hotel by a short, fierce-looking woman with bright, brassy blonde hair. Her lips were covered in bright red lipstick. A cigarette hung from the corner of her mouth. Her eyes were like those of a large fish – blue, but cold. She stared at the children.

"Who's this then?" she said.

"Kids from the school, Vee," Old Nosey said. " 'Ere, what you doing in London?"

"We're on holiday," Tessa said. "Staying with my aunty."

"Oh, very nice," Old Nosey said sarcastically. "Ain't it, Wal?"

Wally curled his lip up and muttered, "No."

"We're just off to the shops," Old Nosey went on.

"Yes," Mrs Harding said. "Spend! Spend! Spend! That's my motto!"

"'Ere!" Old Nosey cried. "Don't you go spending all my hard-earned cash!"

"I'll spend what I like!" Mrs Harding said, and clutched her big plastic handbag to her stomach.

"Where's that Leyla got to?" Old Nosey said.

"She's coming," Mrs Harding said. "Just got to put her face on."

A moment later, the hotel door swung open once more, and out of it walked Wally's older sister, Leyla. She was wearing bright red lipstick. Her face was glistening with orange foundation. She clattered towards them in a pair of high-heeled shoes which made her look as if she was standing on tip toe.

"Hey," William whispered as he floated about a metre in the air, "that gel looks more like a ghost than me!"

"You ready, Leyla?" Old Nosey barked. "Don't want another two hours do you, by any chance? Eh?"

Leyla came up to the group.

"Hiya, Tessa. What are you doing here?"

Tessa explained.

"I hope there's no more of them school kids round here," Old Nosey said. "Be picking up litter day and night, I will! Not that there ain't enough already. Just look at it!" He pointed at the chip papers and cartons lying in the gutters.

"Fancy coming shopping?" Leyla said to Tessa. "All girls together?"

"Er ... no thanks," Tessa said. "I've got... We've got…"

"Got to go and see somebody, urgently," Roddy said.

"We're going to the really big shops," Leyla said. "Be lovely, won't it Aunt Ventura?"

Mrs Harding smiled at Tessa. "Come on, missy, come shopping. It's much better than anything else, ain't it, Leyla?"

"I wanna look at trainers, I do," Wally said. "And then go and have the biggest plate of chips and burgers I can find!"

"Yeah. So do I," Old Nosey said. "Come on. Let's get on with it!" He began to march down the street, with Wally right beside him.

"Ah, well, dear," Mrs Harding said, "you don't know what you're missing, does she, Leyla?"

"See you, Tessa," Leyla said. "You must be a

very sad person if you don't like shops. That's all *I* can say!"

"What a cheek!" Tessa said as they walked away.

"Come on," William said, "we haven't got time to waste on a few stray words from the likes of her. I want to find *that house* again and that little horrible creep, De-Sniff."

"But fancy them being here! A whole bunch of Hardings and Crabbes!" Tessa groaned. "It's like a horror movie!"

"Here, hold my hands," William said. "Let's go flying!"

Tessa and Roddy nipped into a small alleyway and took hold of William's spectral hands. At once they became invisible and as William rose into the sky, so did they.

Chapter 15

Gothic House

At once the river came into better focus. They had a bird's-eye view of it. The road, next to it, now looked narrower. They could see Old Nosey strolling along in his sports jacket. Wally walked next to him. He was clicking away with a camera.

"Just our luck to get him *and* Wally right on the doorstep!" Roddy said.

"I can't see no island," William cried as he peered along the ribbon of water. He flew up higher and edged out to a point halfway across the river. He hovered in the air. Roddy and Tessa, still holding his hands, went with him. Beneath them boats moved up and down evenly on the swell of the big river. The air was noticeably fresher above the water. They could smell no trace of the warm, diesel-fumed atmosphere of the London streets up here.

"Let's head west," Roddy said. "But go slowly so that we don't miss the island. It must be fairly well-hidden, and it was really pretty small, wasn't it?"

They flew downstream for a long way, but they couldn't see the house anywhere.

They flew lower, skimming over the rigging and funnels of boats; they flew higher, they flew this way and back the way they'd come, but nowhere could they see the house they were searching for.

And then Tessa let out a yell.

"Over there! Look!"

The boys stared up and down the river, but they couldn't see anything except a couple of boats making their way towards the sea, which was far away.

"Not at the river," Tessa cried. "Over there!"

William and Roddy glanced round and at first saw a brightly painted yellow wall. But near to it was a battered old white van. It was parked half up on the pavement next to a lamppost. There was something in the untidy way it was parked that instantly struck them.

"It's De-Sniff's," Tessa shrieked above the wind. "I'm sure of it!"

"You're right," William said, as they landed next to it. "I'd know that rotting heap anywhere!"

Roddy and Tessa had let go of William's hands so they were visible again.

"Let's look inside," Tessa said. She tried the door handle. It wouldn't budge. She began wrenching at it with all her might.

"What are you two up to? Is that your van?" A man who was passing shouted. He looked angry and came towards them.

"It belongs to…" Tessa was saying, but just at that moment, William slipped his hand in hers and Roddy's and they both became invisible.

"Eh?" the man said. "Where you hiding, eh? Come on!" He looked under the van. Then he walked three times round it, then he looked under it again and then he peered inside as well. He stood on the pavement scratching his head.

"Blimey," he said. "Must be going off me head!"

He still kept looking around the van though.

"Ruddy awful parking!" he muttered. "And just look at the state of those tyres!" Then he went on his way with many a look back over his shoulder.

As soon as they could, the children tried the other doors. All were locked.

"Hang on a minute," William said. "Keep down, out of sight, while I take a look."

He floated through the side of the van with no effort at all. A few moments later he came out again.

"Anything there?" Roddy said.

"Nah. Just junk, as usual."

"No jars?" Tessa said.

"Only empty ones," William said, sadly. "But there are signs that he's still trying to collect ghosts. There's some Ghost Immobilizing Vapour in there as well."

"The van being here means De-Sniff must have something to do with the old house," Roddy said.

"And if Eric's not in the van," William said, looking out towards the river, "then he could well be in the house!"

"But where is it?" Roddy said, turning round to search the river once more.

"Can you remember anything which stood out when we were pulled here by the brushes?" Tessa said. "Any landmark which caught your eye?"

Roddy thought about it. He went back in his mind, imagining himself and Tessa roaring over the land, then sweeping down towards the river. The lights were on his right. But they had been flying west. Now they had turned about they'd already found De-Sniff's van.

"I think we must be very close," Roddy said. "But we should be flying that way." He pointed in the direction of some large glass buildings. He glanced at his watch. "We ought to be getting back. It's nearly teatime already and Mum and Dad'll start getting worried if we don't turn up soon."

"Let's take another gander then. Quick!" William said. He held out his hands and as soon as Tessa and Roddy held them, they whizzed up into the sky once more. Over bridges they flew – they could see Big Ben, Westminster and Nelson's Column in the distance. They flew over the National Theatre, cutting off a corner of the river, and flew on towards Blackfriars Bridge. As they flew, they kept their eyes peeled, looking out for that place, that strange, twisted and ugly house which they knew was there – somewhere!

The river ran on – the sweet Thames – busy with boats, yet majestically cutting through the heaving mass of London.

"My arms are aching!" Tessa called.

They turned round and flew back the way they'd come.

"Where is it?" Roddy shouted.

William brought the three of them down lower and lower towards the river and then Roddy cried out, "Wait! Back there! What was that?"

William swung them round again.

"Where, mate?" he said. "What you seen?"

"Go lower and slower," Roddy called.

They flew at the same level as many of the office blocks and tower buildings which crowded in towards the river. And then, off to one side, they saw a strange spur, cutting away from the main flow.

A little way along a small inlet there was an island, and on the island was a hideous old mansion.

"That's it!" Tessa shrieked. "I remember that tower now!"

William circled the place slowly. Round and round the turrets he flew, close to the crumbling stonework and the large walls as they rose up out of the rock. It was a dreadful place, with tiny barred windows and horrible griffins round the roof and over the doors. Spindly weeds and bushes were poking out of some of the cracks. The river lapped gently against the rocks on which it stood.

"Wow!" Tessa hissed. "It's awesome."

They circled slowly downwards. In the daylight, it seemed even more massive than it had at night.

Roddy turned and looked at his sister. She was biting her lip.

"I don't like it," she shouted above the wind. "And we ought to be getting back!"

"It's horrible!" William whispered. "Horrible and yet familiar."

"You mean you recognize it?" Tessa said.

"Yeah. I do. It's from me past life. I ain't sure why, but I just know it is. Blimey, it's making me hair crawl."

It was true, William's hair was crawling off his scalp and kept floating away, only to return a few moments later.

"It's worse inside, though," Roddy yelled.

"I gotta get Eric and we gotta get them brushes!"

"Let's go back, first," Tessa cried. "I'm worried about Flora. And Mum and Dad will be wondering where we are!"

"She's right," Roddy said. "Now we know where it is, we can come back."

William circled the place again.

"I ought to go in, mates. I gotta save Eric, I have!"

"You don't know he's in there! Let's go back to Aunty Marion's first," Tessa yelled.

Reluctantly, William wheeled away from the ancient mansion and flew rapidly along the river with Roddy on one side of him and Tessa on the other.

Soon they found Aunty Marion's house and landed right outside it. They were just about to go when they heard a familiar voice. It was Wally. But they couldn't see him anywhere.

Aunty Marion's front door was ajar, so Tessa went quickly inside the house, followed by Roddy and of course, the ghostly shoeshine boy. They found themselves in the lovely hallway with its tumbling flowers and pretty vases.

"Hello, my dears," their aunt said. "Oh, I am glad you've come back just now."

Roddy and Teresa smiled appreciatively at their aunt. But as they turned round they got a shock. Their aunty smiled.

"Look who's here, she said. "Your friend."

Roddy spluttered when he saw none other than Wally Crabbe standing behind the door.

"W-wally?" he gasped.

"I've been hearing wht *good* friends you two are!" Aunty Marion said. "Wally's been telling me all about how you get on so well at school."

"He has?" Tessa said.

"Yes," Aunty Marion smiled. "And how *fortunate* that he has come to London on holiday too, and only staying virtually next door!"

"Yeah, brilliant," Roddy muttered. "Absolutely brilliant! I don't think."

"Well, I was just outside when I bumped into your nice school caretaker, Mr Harding and his family. And, well, I've invited them in for a cup of tea."

Roddy and Tessa reluctantly followed their aunt and Wally into the sitting room. Old Nosey, Mrs Harding and Leyla were sitting there as if they'd moved in.

"Hello, young 'un," Old Nosey said, smiling. "Didn't expect to see us, eh?"

"Er ... no," Roddy said.

"It was so lucky to just meet in the road like that," Aunty Marion said.

"Yeah," Old Nosey laughed. "Was, wannit? Lucky you dropped your bag and I bent down and picked it up, eh?"

"Oh no," Tessa whispered.

"Lovely house you got here." Old Nosey began.

"Very nice," Mrs Harding was saying as she made herself comfortable next to Mr Oliver.

There wasn't really room for them all to sit down in the room, so Aunty Marion said, "Look, why don't you show Leyla and Wally your rooms?"

Roddy very nearly choked on his cake. He and Tessa led Leyla and Wally up the stairs silently.

"Why grown-ups have to be so daft," Wally said, "I don't know."

"Because that's what you call manners," Leyla replied grandly.

"Huh," Wally said. "I didn't want to come here, anyway! Just because Uncle Jake accidentally bumped into their aunty and got talking!"

"You don't want that Wally geezer here!" William said in Roddy's ear. "Why don't yer chuck him out?"

"Ssh," Roddy said.

"What you on about, Oliver?" Wally said, just as if they were still at school. "Not still talking to yourself, are you, daft bat?"

"No, I'm talking to the ethereal orders," Roddy said, using a phrase he'd heard his mother use.

"Yeah, right!" Wally laughed. "You've got a screw loose you have."

Suddenly Flora swept into the room. Tessa stared at her, hoping she wasn't going to cause trouble. But Flora just hovered about in the air looking at Wally and Leyla.

"Who's that?" she asked William. "Can they see me?"

"Nah," William said. "It's just a couple of kids what know Roddy and Tessa."

"When we going to the orphanage, then?" Flora said to Roddy.

"Hang on a minute," he replied, without Wally or Leyla hearing him.

Flora almost flew into a rage at Roddy's answer, then thought better of it. She flew up to the curtain rail and sat there, glaring at everybody.

Leyla and Tessa were talking about clothes and rings.

"I'd love to have my tongue pierced in three places," Leyla was saying. "It's so cool, isn't it?"

"I should think it hurts," Tessa said.

"I'll do anything for fashion, I will," Leyla replied. "I'd even lie down in front of a bus and let it run over me if I thought it would make me look good."

Tessa raised her eyebrows at Roddy, and Roddy smirked.

"I've bin run over by a carriage," William muttered, "and I tell you this, Roddy, it ain't no fun. That gel there don't know what she's talking about."

" 'Ere, what you up to anyway?" Wally said to Roddy. "This holiday, I mean."

"Might go exploring," Roddy said evasively. "What about you?"

"Exploring?" Wally sneered. "You're a duff git, Oliver, you are! Fancy coming to London and then doing that!"

"I suppose you'll be doing something much more interesting," Roddy said angrily.

"We're being called," Leyla said as Aunty Marion's voice rang up the stairs.

"Yeah, well, see you around," Wally said. "And if you find summat good to do, don't forget us, will you?" He gave Roddy a nasty smile and went hurrying out of the room with Leyla.

"That geezer wants a good punch up the lughole!" William said. "He's got no manners at all, he ain't!"

As soon as Wally and Leyla had gone, Flora flew

down and started on again about wanting to go to the orphanage.

"You promised!" she said.

"And I've got to go back to that house!" William insisted. "I've got no time to waste."

"Waste?" Flora shouted. "Do you call saving my friends 'waste'?"

"No, course not," William sighed. He turned to Tessa.

"Couldn't you just wait a bit longer?" Tessa said. Flora scowled.

"Or you, William. We could go to the house tomorrow, maybe?"

"No!" William huffed. "No!"

"We can't go out until the grown-ups have gone to bed, anyway," Roddy said.

But William was anxiously flying round and round the room, changing size and vanishing through walls and then returning.

"I just wanna go, now! I wanna know what happened to Eric. See if he's all right. And I want them brushes back."

"OK," Roddy said. "But we did promise Flora."

"That's right!" Flora cried. "And I want to go now!"

"Look out," Tessa whispered. "Somebody's coming upstairs."

It was Mrs Oliver. She knocked at the door and came into the room.

"We've decided to go to the theatre," she said. "Would you two like to come?"

"We'd rather not, if you don't mind," Tessa said. "We're a bit tired, aren't we, Roddy?"

"Oh, that's all right," Mrs Oliver said. "You'll be all right, won't you?"

"Fine, Mum!" Tessa said. "I am nearly fourteen, you know!"

William glared at them when their mother had gone.

"That's it then, ain't it? You don't want to come with me, do you?"

"Yes, of course we do," Tessa cried. "As soon as we get back from going with Flora – as we promised. We'll set off then, won't we Roddy?"

"Yeah," Roddy said. "That's a promise.

"And you must come with us," Tessa said.

"No, I ain't going," William said.

"Now who's sulking?" Flora said.

"I ain't sulking!" William shouted.

"Oh, come with us!" Roddy said.

"No." William said. "I'll stop here."

"We won't be long," Roddy said.

"Huh!" William said.

William made himself very small, floated up to the top of the wardrobe and perched there.

Roddy and Tessa heard the front door bang shut.

"They've gone," Tessa said.

"Right then," Flora said, holding out her hands so that Roddy and Tessa could become invisible. "Let's get going. Only remember, this won't be easy. Old Breakham is a real villain and if he catches me, he'll make me suffer."

Chapter 16

The Orphanage

The orphanage was situated on the edge of London, to the east. It was a grim building, now derelict. The main floor was wrapped in the ghostly substance called Ectofirm that couldn't be broken by ordinary ghosts.

It was inside here that Flora's friends were trapped. Each child-ghost had a small floating bed to sleep on. They still wore the same garments they'd died in – mostly rags. Now, as Roddy, Tessa and Flora arrived outside the orphanage, a shadow swept momentarily across Flora. She shook herself and recovered. Purring, Nooby wound his way up her chest and wrapped himself round her neck.

"Come and peep through here," Flora said, as

she gestured towards a chink in the threadbare curtains. Roddy, Tessa and Flora hovered, high up the side of the building, peering inside it.

The ghost children were getting ready for bed. Some of the smaller ones were crying for their parents. Others cursed and raged about being caged up. All in all, it was a miserable place. Cold and damp and lonely. Several of the children knelt down to say their prayers.

"'Urry up, you grovelling little scumbags!" a harsh voice yelled. "I ain't got all night waiting for you to go to bed!"

"It's Breakham," Flora whispered.

A grotesque, fat man appeared at the door of the bare dormitory. He was dressed in cheap Victorian clothes: a waistcoat with a gilt chain across it, a grubby shirt with rolled-up sleeves, baggy trousers with a big belt holding them up. He glowered round the room.

The children fled on to their floating bunks and hid their faces. But after Breakham had gone away, one or two of them whispered, "Good night, sleep tight."

"How do we get them out?" Roddy whispered.

"We've got to get inside first," Flora said.

Tessa looked at Flora curiously, "That'll be easy, surely?"

Flora shook her head.

"Not for a ghost," she replied. "The dormitory is sealed with Ectofirm. I only managed to escape because Nooby found a tiny cat-sized hole in the Ectofirm, got outside and tricked Breakham into opening the door, just long enough for me to flit out."

"There must be a way." Roddy said.

"There is," Flora said, "but it means you'll have to do it."

"What?" Tessa hissed.

"I've been thinking about it," she said. "And the easiest way for you to get inside is to become solid again."

"What about you?" Tessa asked.

"I'll get inside that bottle. And you can take me in, in your pocket."

"What about Breakham?" Roddy said.

"He might try and stop you, but probably he'll just wait for you to leave."

"He won't try and harm us?" Tessa said.

"I don't know," Flora said. "I wouldn't have thought so, because he won't know that you can see him."

137

"I don't feel that keen on testing him out," Tessa said nervously. They were floating about twenty metres in the air on the outside of the derelict building.

"You've got to!" Flora said angrily. "It's the only way!"

Roddy sighed.

"Do you really think it'll work?" he said.

"Yes," Flora replied. "And if you don't help me, those poor creatures will have to stay there for ever!"

"Right," Tessa said suddenly. "We'll do it, won't we, Roddy?"

"Good!" Flora whispered. "Thank you! Thank you both!"

Still holding Roddy's and Tessa's hands, she flew down to the room beneath the dormitory. They passed through the wall and came to rest on an uneven floor.

"The Ectofirm is only wrapped round the floor they're on," she said. She released Roddy's and Tessa's hands and they became solid.

"Look at this!" Roddy hissed. Beneath his feet, the floorboards were splintering and decayed.

"One wrong move and we could fall," Tessa said, looking down through the cracks to the floor below.

"Don't worry," Flora said. "I'll watch you. Just be careful where you tread!" She led them carefully across an open area and up a creaking staircase until they were standing uneasily outside the dirty old door into the dormitory. The floor cracked as Roddy and Tessa stepped on it.

"Quickly," Flora said. "Open the bottle and let me get inside it."

As soon as she was tucked safely inside Roddy's pocket, he pushed open the rickety door. Immediately, some of the child ghosts woke up and stared fearfully at them. At the same time, old Breakham came hurrying out of his own room.

"What the blazes?" he growled. Then he stopped in his tracks. "Bodies?" he gasped. "You lot!" he shouted at the child ghosts. "Don't you move a hair! We don't want no Nosy Parkers in here, investigating."

All the ghosts watched Roddy and Tessa quietly as they gingerly walked into the room.

"This will be fine," Tessa said, pretending she couldn't see the ghosts at all. "We'll just stay here for the night!"

"Perishin' intruders!" Mr Breakham bellowed. "Get back to sleep you lot! It's only a pair of them stupid, modern kids. Be gone by tomorrow! Get back to sleep, I said. And don't any one of yer dare to move, do you hear me?"

The ghost children pretended to settle down. Mr Breakham stayed for a long time though, watching Roddy and Tessa, with evil eyes. Only when he thought they were fast asleep, did he float away into his room once more.

Roddy and Tessa waited. All went very quiet, except for the rats scampering behind the skirting boards and the wind whistling through the broken windows.

When they thought it was safe, Tessa and Roddy sat up and looked around. Almost at once, curious orphans came sweeping towards them, hovering in the air. A few reached out and touched their hair. There was a whispering buzz of excitement. Roddy put his finger to his lips and said, "Ssh," very softly.

The ghost children shot away from them, startled. But then Roddy took the bottle out of his pocket and released Flora.

"They're my friends!" she hissed. The other orphans were astonished and joyful.

"Keep quiet!" Flora urged them. "We don't want Breakham back in here, do we?"

She explained how she had escaped and how Roddy and Tessa had helped.

"Can we get out too?" some of them whispered eagerly.

Flora told them as much as she could in a short time. She told them that she had come back to free them, but that they had to be very, very careful. Her words excited the young ghosts so much they almost forgot about Mr Breakham.

"What was that?" Tessa whispered. There had been a creak from the floor below.

"Not Breakham, I don't think," Flora whispered back.

"It sounds as if someone else has got in," Roddy hissed.

"Who ... who...?" the ghosts asked nervously.

Flora didn't have time to reply. In any case, she was speechless at what she now saw. Entering the room strode a tall woman wearing a long cloak. She had broken through the protective Ectofirm as a solid human and now, as they stared at her, she became invisible herself, just like a ghost.

It was Mrs Croker, and in her hands she held the Ghost Nabber.

"Yes!" she cried, when she saw just how many

young ghosts her compass had led her to. "Yes! Yes! Yes!"

With a start, she noticed Roddy and Tessa.

"You!" she sneered. "Always in the way! Well, you won't stop me this time!"

The ghost children screamed and started running madly round the room. In the confusion, Roddy and Tessa got parted from Flora.

Mr Breakham came rushing out of his room. He was completely astounded by what he saw.

Before he could say a word, Mrs Croker pressed the button on the Ghost Nabber and sucked him into it. The two youngest orphans were next. They zoomed into the Nabber as easy as a wink. This so startled and frightened the others, that they were easy prey. Mrs Croker swept after them, screeching with triumph.

"Got you!" she shouted, each time one of the small ghosts was sucked into the machine. "Got you! Revolting creatures!"

At last, Roddy and Tessa found Flora hiding behind her spectral cat, in a corner.

"Quick!" Tessa hissed at Flora, "get into the bottle!"

Still nabbing the ghost orphans, Mrs Croker

didn't notice Flora and her cat dive into the bottle once more. Nor did she see Roddy and Tessa make for the exit. The next minute, they were running down the rotten steps to the floor below.

"Stop!" Tessa called. Roddy came to a halt. "It's not safe!"

A piece of board had broken under her foot. It clattered down through the building.

"Get Flora out of the bottle!" Tessa commanded.

As Flora appeared, Roddy and Tessa grabbed her hands.

"Get us back to Aunty Marion's," Tessa said. "Quickly! Before the Ghost Hunter comes out!"

Flora didn't need to be asked twice. She zipped through the wall, with Roddy and Tessa hanging on to her like a couple of rag-dolls, and flew like the wind back to 7 Ravenbell Road.

Chapter 17

No Way Out

William had stayed on the top of the wardobe for some time after the others had left for the orphanage. He was remembering how well he and Eric had got on.

Even when I first met him. Even though he was about four hundred years old, I knew he was a real kind old geezer. Like a father to me, he was. Now he's been dragged off, away from Chillwood Castle, wot he loves. And all me mates can do is tell me to wait, wait, wait!

All at once, he made up his mind. He scribbled a note for Roddy and Tessa. Then he flew out of the window, with the roaring traffic below him. He headed back along the river until he reached the small inlet on which the decrepit mansion stood.

He circled it a number of times, feeling nervous. There was something about the place which made his hair tremble and his hands shake.

"It ain't no use just going round and round though is it?" William said to himself. "Come on me boy – what are yer, a boy or a throat lozenge, eh?"

He flew downwards until he was level with a small window in the lower part of the house. He hovered outside it, looking in. The room looked like a kitchen. Inside it, there was a butler, preparing food.

William cautiously entered the room by passing through the wall.

The butler was humming to himself.

William watched him for a few minutes. When he left the kitchen, William followed. There was nobody else about. The butler went into a big sitting room. William peeped round the door, half-expecting to see De-Sniff. The room was empty. As he went in, a strange feeling came over him. He looked up and saw the portrait of Obadiah Quirke staring down at him.

William jumped.

He went up close to the picture and noted the

name written beneath it. Suddenly a horrible feeling came over him. He glanced back at the man's face. It was a face William knew. A face from the past. Prickles of fear ran along William's brow and his floating hair stood up and tried to wander off his scalp.

"Quirke!" he murmured.

The name, once he'd said it, sent shivers of anger and terror through William. It made him remember his own family back in Victorian times. He could see them – his brothers and sisters and his mother weeping in their poor home. But most vividly of all, he saw his father, Albert Povey, broken and alone in Newgate Prison. After Obadiah Quirke had put him there.

Tears came to William's eyes. For a few seconds he could even hear his father's voice speaking to him. The last time William had ever seen him.

The sound of a door sliding open broke into William's thoughts. To his surprise, the butler had moved a bookcase and gone into a room beyond. William followed him cautiously into the room.

Straight away, he saw it was a lab. Nervously, he gaped at all the paraphernalia. As the butler dusted bottles of chemicals, William began to search around to see if there was any sign of Eric or the brushes. The butler finished his work and went out of the lab. While he was standing there, a strange feeling came over William. He was sensing that something nearby belonged to his ghostly world. He crouched down to get nearer to the flow of energy which reached him. He looked between the legs of tables and stools and saw one of his shoe brushes right at the back of a space underneath a table. At once he gathered it up, delighted to have at least *one* of them back.

William noticed there was something big on the workbench, covered in a dark plum-coloured cloth. He lifted up the cloth to see what was under it. William froze when he saw who was there.

"Eric!" he whispered. "Eric?"

His old friend sat inside a large glass globe, his head in his hands, along with a number of other dejected ghosts.

As soon as Eric saw William, he leaped to his feet and began smiling and waving to him. William quickly found a heavy iron bar, intending to smash the globe to smithereens. But as he lifted the bar, Eric shook his head. He feared that smashing it might destroy the ghosts. William put the bar down and tried to hold a conversation with Eric. He could hear nothing his friend said, but Eric was able to hear William. All the other ghosts crowded round Eric in a pale, swirling mass, hoping for escape.

"Was it that geezer De-Sniff what got yer?" William asked.

Eric nodded his head vigorously.

"How am I gonna get you out?" William cried.

Eric started pointing urgently behind William. The door to the laboratory was sliding open as De-Sniff tiptoed in. William ducked under the globe machine. De-Sniff carried the Ghost Nabber.

"Right," De-Sniff said to himself. "I must do this *very carefully*. Got a responsible job for once and I ain't going to muck it up."

With infinite care, De-Sniff connected the Ghost Nabber to the Spectrika. Then he pressed the Blow button. The machine hummed softly. William gawped as a huge mass of child-ghosts were spurted out into the globe. De-Sniff had a smug little smile on his face as he switched the Nabber off and stared into the swirling, misty mass of ghosts before him.

"Yes!" he whispered. "Done it!"

He looked round at the Energy Chair that Mrs Croker had nearly completed making. It was connected by tubes and wires to the Spectrika.

"Ain't fair, though, " he muttered. "Ain't blinkin' fair. I never gets a chance at really exciting things, I don't!"

William saw De-Sniff glance up at the Ghostometer. His eyes grew big. He got very worked up.

"Oh crikey! " De-Sniff shrieked and ran out of the lab.

William floated back quickly to the Spectrika where the new ghosts, along with the ones already in the globe, had now settled into an overcrowded mass. He could just make out Eric, staring towards him. His mouth was moving and his hands were gesturing.

"What is it?" William hissed. "What's De-Sniff up to? Eric?"

Eric was urgently mouthing at William, like a goldfish in a tank. William was concentrating hard, trying to read Eric's lips. He was concentrating so hard in fact that he didn't notice someone come hurrying into the laboratory behind him.

Eric began signalling frantically, pointing and waving his arms about.

"What is it?" William said.

Eventually, he twisted round and saw what Eric meant.

"*The Ghost Hunter!*" he gasped. "*She's still alive!*" He was so scared, he was rooted to the spot.

The Ghost Hunter walked straight towards William. He knew her long nose would pick up his scent any second now, and she would go crazy. But Mrs Croker kept walking across the room. She strode right up to William and then ... then she walked right through him!

"Blimey!" William thought. "She can't smell me!"

Mrs Croker wasn't sniffing at all. Her nose didn't seem the same. It was bruised and battered. And there was a streak of white in her hair, as if she'd had a terrible fright herself.

She stared at the Ghostometer.

"Ninety-eight ghosts! That means I need just one more, De-Sniff!"

"Yeah, boss! Great, ain't it? I done a good job, ain't I, boss, blowin' them in there?"

But Mrs Croker had spotted something else to excite her. It was the Ghost Nabber's light, flashing gently. The light warned that there was a ghost present in the area. Mrs Croker's eyes narrowed dangerously. Cunningly, so as not to cause alarm, she took out the box containing the shoe brush from a bag she had strapped to her waist. Now she opened it calmly and took the brush in her hand. She became invisible, ghostly. Instantly, she came face to face with a startled William.

Just for a moment they examined each other – William almost mesmerized by her fierce, staring eyes – Mrs Croker *so* excited that she almost screamed with joy.

"You!" she cried.

She lifted the Ghost Nabber and pointed it at William.

William realized he was in great danger. With a burst of energy, he zoomed through the ceiling and flew up through layer after layer of the tall house. Mrs Croker screamed in anger and immediately tore after him, her red cloak spreading out behind her as she raced upwards. When William reached the top of the house, Mrs Croker caught up with him.

"There's no escape this time, boy!" she howled.

William dived downwards towards the river, swooping and dodging in every way he could. He plunged into the stony hill, through many layers, deep into the earth, but still Mrs Croker followed him. When he could go no further, he turned and scorched back up again. And still Mrs Croker flew after him.

"I've got you, Povey!" she laughed. "Wherever you go, whatever you do, I shall be there!" Her face had a mad expression as she whirled close to the terrified boy. He dived again, twisting crazily, darting and ducking, swivelling and swirling. He tried every trick he knew.

"No escape, Povey!" she cried hysterically. "No escape!"

Chapter 18

Gone to Deadlock Hall

When Roddy and Tessa got back to Aunty Marion's from the orphanage, they were shaking.

"My friends!" Flora whined. "All lost to that horrible, evil woman!"

"She's worse than ever!" Roddy said. "Did you see her eyes?"

"Where's Will?" Flora shouted.

"Don't know," Tessa said. She was sitting on the bed, picking pieces of broken wood out of her trainers.

"He's not here!" Roddy cried.

Tessa sprang to her feet. She looked under the bed and up at the top of the wardrobe, where William usually dozed.

"William!" she called softly. "William!"

"Where d'you think he's gone?" Flora asked.

"I'll give you one guess!" said Roddy.

"You mean he's gone to the Ghost Hunter's place?"

"Yes," Tessa said. Suddenly she saw a note on the dressing table, held down by a vase:

Gon to Croke's. Won't be longe. Had too goe. W.

"Well, what are we waiting for?" Flora cried. "Let's get after him! And with a bit of luck we might find my friends as well!"

"We've got to be careful, " Roddy said. "The Ghost Hunter ... she's *really* dangerous now, and anyway we can't go to Deadlock Hall spectrally because she's got that machine, *and* she can see ghosts!"

"Well, I'm going by myself," Flora said firmly.

"No, wait," Tessa said quickly. "Do you want to end up like your friends?"

"Look," Roddy said. "William said in this note he'd be back soon. That means we've got to wait for him. It's absolutely no use us going off chasing after him, putting ourselves at risk, when he might even be on his way back!"

"I want my friends!" Flora said.

"We all want that!" Roddy cried. "But we just have to work it out carefully! Why don't we wait and see if William comes back first? If he isn't here by early morning, we'll go after him."

"If we go as we are, not as ghosts," Tessa said, "we could carry you and Nooby in the bottle in Roddy's pocket, and then there'd be far less danger for all of us!"

Flora flopped down on the bed. "You won't let me down, will you?" she whispered. Then suddenly she burst into tears. Ghostly pearls dropped from her eyes and landed on the bed. Nooby crawled from her pocket and climbed up to her shoulder. He miaowed with concern and began licking her face. Tessa also went and put her arm round Flora.

"Don't worry," she said. "If William isn't here by tomorrow morning, we'll go after him and your friends."

Roddy ran quickly with Tessa along the pavement towards the bus stop, amidst the roar of morning

London traffic. Flora and Nooby were tucked safely inside his jacket pocket.

They didn't realize it, but as they hurried along, somebody was watching them. As soon as they caught the bus, the watcher ran up and got on it as well. Roddy and Tessa were on the upper deck; the person following them sat out of sight, on the lower one. When the bus finally stopped at Roddy and Tessa's stop, the watcher got off as well, hidden amongst a crowd of people.

Roddy and Tessa crossed the road and came to the river embankment. They were next to the shallow reach of water away from the main river. It was just a short distance to Deadlock Hall.

Luckily they found a place nearby with boats for hire. When they asked if they could hire one, the young man looked them up and down.

"You ever bin on a boat before?" he said.

"Yes," Tessa said. "We've been on boating holidays a few times and we know how to row, don't we Roddy?"

"Yes," Roddy agreed.

"Where d'you want to go?" the man asked.

"To that island, possibly," Roddy said.

"What for?"

"No particular reason," Tessa said.

"OK," the man said. "Never liked that place though. You be careful up there, now. It's haunted, I reckon!" He began to chuckle gently.

"It'll cost you a fiver. It's pretty safe on this leg of the river, but don't go into the main one, will you?"

"No, of course not," Tessa said.

Tessa paid and the man held the boat steady as they climbed into it. Roddy rowed them across the narrow piece of water until they reached a shallow shingle shelf. They heaved the boat up on to it and tethered it with a stone.

"What now?" Tessa said.

"Now we just walk in and find William, of course!" Roddy said.

Tessa pulled a face at him.

"I am not going back in through that cellar. We'll have to try another way."

"And how do you think we'll do that?" Roddy said sharply.

Tessa sighed.

"I don't know. But we've got to get in somehow!"

They began to walk up the rocky hill. It was very difficult and they had to get on hands and knees and climb in some places. At last, Tessa sat down with a bump on some coarse grass.

"I'm tired out!" she panted. She swept back her red hair. It was nearly as red as her hot face.

Roddy sat down next to her. The sun was shining strongly.

"Me too," he said glaring at the huge building. "There must be an easy way to get in. There must!"

Chapter 19

Inside the Hall of Doom

The person who had been following Roddy and Tessa down the road and on the bus had also watched them as they hired a boat. He had watched them row over to the strange-looking island with the odd-looking house on top of it. That person was Wally Crabbe.

"Hey, mate, what's that place then?" he asked the boatman.

"Don't tell me you want to go there an' all!" the boatman said. "It costs five quid there and back."

"Five quid?" he said. "What is it? A theme park or summat?"

The boatman looked round at Wally. His tattooed arms rippled with muscles.

"No, it's just a broken-down old house that's been there for years."

Wally stood gazing across the water at the island. He knew Roddy and Tessa were up to something.

"Can you let me have a boat for a quid?" he said. "That's all I've got."

The boatman laughed.

"No way! What d'you think I am? A charity or something?"

Wally felt around in his pockets.

"What about three pounds?" he said. "I really haven't got any more. And it's better than nothing, isn't it?"

The man was shaking his head and laughing.

"You're worse than that miser in Oliver Twist, you are, what's his name?"

"Is it a deal, then?" Wally said.

"Can you row?" the man said.

"What? Well ... yeah. I can row. I've done rowing. It's easy, ain't it?"

"Come on then, cheapskate," the boatman said.

Wally jumped into the boat so heavily he nearly over-turned it.

"Steady on!" the man said. "You want a shipwreck as well?"

"Can I pay you later?" Wally said.

"If you don't cough up that money now, young un, I'm gonna chuck you in that swamp there and leave you to swim back, right?"

Wally, who understood that kind of message only too well, handed over the three pounds. Then he took up the oars as the man gave the boat a push out into the river.

At first Wally kept going round in circles because he was pulling too hard on the right-hand oar. The boatman shouted instructions from the bank.

"I'm all right," Wally shouted back hotly. "I know what I'm doing!"

Wally whacked the water with the oars, as if he was angry with it.

"Get on!" he shouted at the boat. Gradually, he got a bit better at using the oars and the boat began to move towards the island. Sweaty and flustered, Wally brought the small boat into very shallow water. He immediately sprang out, landing up to his knees in mud.

"Ugh!" he bellowed.

Wally tied up the boat and then, after emptying water from his trainers, began climbing up the rocks of the island, just as Tessa and Roddy had done.

"What them two want to come here for, I dunno!" Wally gasped. He was now very sticky and his face was like a big red apple. "Pair of idiots."

After a while, he came near to the place where Tessa and Roddy were taking a breather.

"What was that?" Tessa said.

"It's somebody coming this way," Roddy said. "Hide!"

They had just got behind a large rock, when Wally came into view.

When he'd gone past, Tessa said, "What's he doing here?"

"I don't know!" Roddy replied. "He must have followed us all the way from Aunty Marion's!"

"Talk about nosey!" Tessa said. "Worse than his uncle!"

"We ought to get after him," Roddy said. "In case he gives us away to Croker or De-Sniff!"

They scrambled up the hillside now and eventually came to more level ground, with a short pathway up to the huge oak front door of the house. To their amazement, Wally was trying to peep in through its keyhole.

"He'll get a nasty shock if he rings the bell," Tessa whispered.

But Wally began trying the door handle. Then he began pushing hard at the door with his shoulder. Suddenly he turned away. He had a scared expression on his face. A strange clumping sound filled the air. Round the side of the house plodded a weird patrolling robot – obviously another of Mrs Croker's inventions. It was big, with two legs and two arms. Its chest was armour-plated and its head looked like a metal box. It also looked extremely dangerous.

"Intruder noted," its squeaky mechanical voice said.

When Wally saw the armour-plated guard, he let out a nervous little cry. Suddenly the guard launched a spiked steel ball at him. It flew through the air and nearly parted his hair.

Wally squealed like a pig and dived for cover. He ran towards some bushes at the edge of the drive, but the guard followed on its big ungainly feet. Plod! Plod!

"Come on," Roddy said, "we'd better try and help the twit!"

They quickly broke from their own hiding place and chased after the guard and Wally. As they came round the side of the house, though, they were just in time to see Wally hurtling down the hillside. He was going at a terrific pace. Towards the bottom, he fell over and rolled and rolled through bushes until he hit the water with a splash! He lay still.

"Is he hurt?" Tessa gasped in a horrified voice.

"No," Roddy said. "Look."

Wally now got unsteadily to his feet, staggered to the boat and began to row back across the river like a demon.

"What happened to the guard?" Tessa said. They looked all around them, but it was nowhere to be seen.

"Over there," Tessa said. She pointed at big footprints leading towards the house. They followed them for a little way. The footsteps came to a wall and stopped.

"Where did it go?" Roddy said nervously.

"I don't know," Tessa said. "But it was horrible, wasn't it?"

Roddy looked at the wall.

"I think it must have gone through here," he said. He put his hand on the wall to see if he could make out an entrance.

"It's probably still in there," Tessa said. "Don't let it out again!"

Roddy said, "But why did it go back? My guess is it's only programmed to follow one route."

"What d'you mean?" Tessa said.

"There's probably some kind of sensor which activates the guard, and allows it to track the intruder to a certain distance, and when the intruder moves beyond that, it gives up and goes back to its kennel."

"But why didn't it go for us?" she said.

"Probably because there's a sensor by the front door which picked Wally up. We stayed out of its range."

"Look!" Tessa hissed. "I've found a switch!"

A tiny button was hidden among the rocks in the wall. "Don't touch it!" she said.

"It might let us in," Roddy said.

"But the guard will attack us!" Tessa cried. "Don't be an idiot!"

"I don't think it will," Roddy said.

"What d'you mean?" Tessa said. "I suppose you think it's just gone in there to have a nice quiet nap, or something."

"No, of course not," Roddy said. "But just think about it. That guard is a robot and robots only do what they're programmed to do.

"But we don't know what it's programmed to do!" Tessa shuddered.

"No, listen, Tess," Roddy said urgently. "If it's only activated by the sensor over the door, what would that mean?"

"That it's shut down now?"

"Exactly what I think," Roddy said, and without another word he pressed the button in the wall.

"You raving nink!" Tessa cried, and began running away as a door in the wall slid open.

When no robot came rushing out, Tessa went back, cautiously.

At first neither she nor Roddy could make out the inside of the room at all, because it was dark. They went inside.

The robot guard was standing erect in a corner, with its head clamped into a headset. It was quite still.

"Wow!" Tessa whispered as they gazed at the steel arms and legs and the odd steel head.

Roddy crossed the room and switched off the plug which kept the robot's batteries charged.

"Just in case," he said.

The room was dank and musty, like the rest of Deadlock Hall.

"Is there a way inside the rest of the house?" Tessa said.

Roddy was pointing to a door.

"Better close the outside door first," he said. After he'd done that, he and Tessa nervously opened the door from the guard's room into a passageway.

There was a staircase leading down.

"Come on," Roddy whispered. "We've got to find out where Croker's keeping the orphans. Most probably, William will be there as well."

Chapter 20

The Great Experiment

Mrs Croker was cackling with delight when she got back to the lab. She put the shoe brush back in its glass box and became visible. Then she unhooked the Ghost Nabber from her belt, placed it with even greater care than before on to the bench and turned to De-Sniff.

"This is my hour, De-Sniff!" she cried.

"What hour's that then, boss?" De-Sniff said. "Not your *witching* hour, I hope."

"Don't be ridiculous," she snapped. "This is my hour of triumph, my hour of the future and the past! My hour of breaking the barriers which separate worlds. I shall be free of time, De-Sniff. Free of everything!"

"Free of me?" he whispered. He gave a big,

disgusting sniff and wiped his nose on the handkerchief Horace had given him. "I wish I could come, boss. It ain't fair."

"Of course it's not fair! It isn't fair that I was born clever and you were born brainless, is it? Anyway, I won't be gone for ever. I shall be back."

"When you going then, boss?" De-Sniff asked.

"Soon," Mrs Croker said. "Very, very soon. Now come and give me a hand."

"But you haven't got enough of 'em yet, have yer, boss? Ghosts, I mean?" he glanced up at the Ghostometer.

Mrs Croker gave a sneer.

"Oh, I think I have everything I need now, De-Sniff. Yes!"

De-Sniff's eyes widened.

"You caught another, have you?"

"I have caught *the best one of all*," she hissed.

"You haven't!" De-Sniff whispered.

Mrs Croker moved forwards and attached the Nabber to the Spectrika. She pressed the **Blow** button. The machine whirred for a second, then blew out a trail of white particles. The particles swirled into the globe. De-Sniff pressed his face up against it to get a better view. And then he saw...

"*The shoeshine boy!* You got him!" De-Sniff yelled. He turned round with his arm held up in a clenched fist salute.

"Yes!" Mrs Croker cried. "I've got him!"

De-Sniff smirked.

"That's brill, boss, that is."

William sat next to Eric. He was looking very miserable now.

"Will, lad," Eric said.

"I came to save you," William said sadly, "and she got me. After everything! She got me!"

"There, lad. Don't you take on now," Eric said. "You did your best, didn't you. Can't do no more 'n that."

"We're done for," William said. "We'll never get out of here in one piece."

"Aye, well," Eric said. He put his arm round William's shoulders. "What will be will be, young un, won't it?"

"Come here," Mrs Croker shouted across the room to her assistant as he watched the ghosts.

De-Sniff went over to where she was standing.

"Hold this," she passed him a large spanner. "I

want to check out the arrangements of the chair."

De-Sniff looked at the Energy Chair – a chair which looked as if it had come out of a space rocket. It was connected to the Spectrika by a set of tubes and wires. She began fiddling with it, making adjustments and tightening bolts.

"What's this button do, boss?" De-Sniff asked, pointing at a large green one at the front of the chair.

"Don't touch that!" Mrs Croker yelled.

"Sorry, guv," De-Sniff said. "I only wanted…"

"Well don't," Mrs Croker snapped. "That button is the start button, and if you press that before it's time, I don't know what will happen. You could ruin everything. Like you almost did before!"

De-Sniff grimaced. But he stared hard at the green button.

"So that's the one you press when everything's ready. When you got enough energy and that from them ghosts?"

"Quite," Mrs Croker grunted.

"And then you go back in time and never have to worry about dying ever."

"You've got it at last," Mrs Croker said. "I want

to go back to Victorian London when my great-grandfather was alive.

"That Obadiah fella?"

"Yes, De-Sniff. When my family was important in this city!"

"Oh," De-Sniff said. "So they was rich?"

"Yes," Mrs Croker cried. "Now shut up!"

She continued to work on the chair.

The Spectrika was full of ghosts, so full that it resembled a white cloud in which could occasionally be seen individual faces. She had now disconnected the antenna, which had first pulled the brushes to her. It was no longer needed and it had been so badly damaged by De-Sniff that, as yet, she was unable to repair it.

The Ghostometer showed that there were exactly ninety-nine spirits trapped in the Spectrika, which meant that it was ready for her great experiment to begin.

Through the bookcase door, which had been left open, De-Sniff could just see the face of Mrs Croker's great-grandfather, Obadiah, staring at him from the painting on the wall. A creepy feeling came over him and he turned his back on it.

De-Sniff watched and waited. He was growing

bored. But at last Mrs Croker said, "I'm nearly ready, De-Sniff, but I have to go to my room and fetch some things to take with me on my journey."

"What?" De-Sniff said. "You going now, boss? This exact minute?"

"Very soon," Mrs Croker snapped. "As soon as I'm ready."

"But … but …" De-Sniff stammered, "what about me?"

"What *about* you?" the Ghost Hunter grimaced. "I haven't spent all this time working on these things for *you*!"

De-Sniff stared at her. He gave a little sniff. "Righto, boss," he said. "I'll keep me eye on the Hall while you're gone."

"And don't touch a thing, do you hear me, De-Sniff?"

"Don't touch a thing," De-Sniff replied. "Oh, no, I won't boss. I won't touch the brush and I won't touch me own nose. Anything else you don't want me to touch?"

"Don't be ridiculous, De-Sniff," Mrs Croker said. "The brush will be going with me. And keep away from that switch!"

"Why would *I* want to travel through time?" De-Sniff murmured.

"Exactly," Mrs Croker sneered. "You've got enough on your plate living in the present."

She moved towards the door, turning round once to stare lovingly at the Time Machine she had created. Then she went up to her bedroom.

As soon as she had gone, De-Sniff approached the Energy Chair and examined it more closely. He tried to stop himself touching it, but he couldn't help just stroking the leather of the arms a little, and he couldn't help wondering if it really would work.

"Time," he muttered to himself. And he thought about what it might be like to go back to the time when he was born and then to see how he'd been brought up. He knew where he'd lived, but his parents had thrown him out of the house when he was young because they said he was a nuisance. Ever since then, he'd been on his own, living in ditches, eating out of dustbins – until he'd met Mrs Croker.

De-Sniff glanced over his shoulder to make sure Mrs Croker was gone and then he scrambled up into the seat of the Energy Chair.

Just to see what it feels like, he thought to himself. But as soon as he got into the chair, he began to say, "Why shouldn't I go and time travel? I should be the boss, now. If she hadn't have come back, I would have been. Why do I always have to be second fiddle, eh?"

He glanced at the Ghostometer. It read **FULL**. He glanced at the Spectrika. All the ghostly crowd was still swirling around. He gazed at the green button, which had the word **ACTIVATE** on it. Suddenly, De-Sniff reached round and fastened the safety belt.

"Don't see why I shouldn't," he muttered crossly. "Yeah, why shouldn't I?"

Chapter 21

Gone with the Wind

Roddy and Tessa scrambled down the creaking staircase. They didn't realize it, but it would soon be too late to do anything to save their friend.

They passed portraits and dank tapestries and broken furniture. They heard scratching and pattering behind the panelling. A bat skimmed over Tessa's head.

"Ooh! I hate this place," she whispered.

"So do I," Roddy said. His hand slid in some slime on the banister. He shoved back huge cobwebs and flinched when a couple of big black spiders rushed past his nose.

As they reached the hallway, they could hear someone whistling in the kitchen. Tessa put a finger to her lips. They crept along without speaking. Eventually, they reached the sitting room door. Roddy looked into the room, and quickly spotted the bookcase, which still stood open revealing Mrs Croker's lab.

De-Sniff was sitting in a weird contraption, his hand poised over a green button, muttering to himself. He didn't notice the children slip into the lab and hide behind a tall armchair.

"Why shouldn't I?" De-Sniff suddenly yelled, and he pressed the green **Activate** button.

For a moment nothing happened. De-Sniff looked puzzled. He banged the button again, harder.

Then the machinery sprang into life. The power packs fired up, the Spectrika began to whizz. Roddy caught a glimpse of William's terrified face, as he and the rest of the ghosts inside the globe whirled round faster and faster. Lights began flashing all over the machinery. De-Sniff, who had laughed happily at first, now looked very scared.

Roddy darted to the bench. He saw the weird device Mrs Croker had been using at the orphanage. He didn't know it was called a Ghost Nabber. All he knew was that it sucked the ghosts into it. He turned it over. There were various switches. One of them said **Blow** and the other read **Suck**. His hands were fumbling as he tried to fasten the device to the Spectrika by a nozzle at its end.

Just as he had nearly got it in place, the Nabber was seized from his hands and a towering, powerful Mrs Croker knocked him down on to the floor.

"You again!" she screamed at the children. She glared fiercely at them, her eyes now as hard and black as coal. But she turned away from them, to vent her fury on De-Sniff who was lying back in the Energy Chair.

With a tremendous howl, she hurled herself towards it, jumped on to the chair and tried to throttle him.

"You cheating idiot!" she cried. "Trying to steal my invention and my ghosts and my life-line to eternity!"

De-Sniff babbled, and tried to push her off.

"Get away, boss," he said. "It's going unstable. It's gonna blow up!"

"You fool!" she shrieked, grabbing him by the hair. She tried to force him out of the seat, but De-Sniff was soundly strapped in.

"It won't work now, anyway," De-Sniff yelled. "Not with two of us on board!."

"It won't make any difference, you moron," Mrs Croker growled. "Once the reaction has begun, nothing can stop it. Nothing!"

"I'm feeling weird," De-Sniff yelled. "Get off! I'm getting dizzy and really sick. I'm seeing ghosts everywhere! Get off!" He tried to shove Mrs Croker backwards but that only made her fiercer than ever. She grabbed De-Sniff in a vice-like headlock and tried heaving him out of the belt. The Energy Chair had begun wobbling crazily now and was engulfed in a cloud of fumes and strange spooky gases.

"It's mine!" Mrs Croker yelled.

"No, it ain't," De-Sniff gargled from the side of his mouth. "It's mine an' all!"

"No!"

"Yes!"

"No!" De-Sniff snuffled in the headlock.

"Yes! Yes!" Mrs Croker screamed, more crazily than ever.

As the wobbling and shaking of the Energy Chair grew worse, the children, rooted to the spot, wondered what to do.

"Get Flora out of the bottle!" Tessa called. "She might be able to help us."

Quickly, Roddy took the bottle from his pocket and Flora flew out of it and grew to full size. She was horrified to see what was happening.

"We can't get the ghosts out of there!" Tessa yelled pointing at the globe. Flora flew towards it but she couldn't do anything either. The Spectrika itself was shaking like a tree in a storm and there seemed no way the ghosts in it could be saved.

The Energy Chair began vibrating and wobbling even faster – so fast that it looked as if it was in danger of shaking itself to bits. De–Sniff and Mrs Croker were nothing but blurred shapes whizzing backwards and forwards. But the Ghost Hunter went on howling at her assistant like someone who has gone completely berserk.

And then it happened. There was a groaning deep in the basement of the old house; a quaking and moaning and quivering of unearthly proportions. It was followed at once by a flash of piercing yellow light, which shot from the Spectrika to the Energy Chair and created an explosion of energy in the centre of the room.

With the explosion came a smell of roses, as the floor began to melt into a round, glowing, glimmering hole, its edges peeling back on themselves like clouds before a hurricane. There was a terrific force of wind which swept round the room, knocking things over, swirling objects against walls, hurling debris through windows and yet also drawing other things towards it like a huge sucking nozzle.

Roddy and Tessa felt their bodies lifted from the floor and whizzed round and round. The Spectrika suddenly split open like an over-ripe melon down one of its intricate seams. The ghosts inside were sprayed out all over the place. Mr Breakham wobbled like a huge jelly and flaked out across the workbench.

Many of the orphans were affected in the same way and lay around, as if they'd been knocked out. Flora flew round to them in turn, coaxing them to get up and to get away.

"Come on!" she squealed. "Hurry! Before Breakham gets his miserable guts back together and starts rounding you up. Quick!"

The orphans found it very difficult to find any energy. It was as if they'd been robbed of their own.

"Please try!" Flora cried to them. "Please!"

Many of the orphans just lay, looking up at her.

Flora tried yanking them to their feet and tried to make them move.

"Hurry!" she cried. She kept glancing over her shoulder to see how Breakham was doing. He too was finding it difficult to enliven himself. He looked like a balloon that had lost all its gas. He lay twitching and groaning. Gradually the young ghosts struggled to their feet and made themselves float upwards again. Flora watched them as they reached the wall and passed through it.

Even Eric was able to come round as William went up to him.

"Oh, so good to be out of there, eh, Will?"

"Yeah," William said to his old friend. "Now you better get going, me old mate. Go back to Chillwood and I'll come and see you one of these days, eh?"

"Be very good," Eric said. " 'Tis an age since I've been near the place and I thought I'd never see it again!" He looked round at the mayhem that Croker and De-Sniff had created.

"Go, quickly!" William urged.

Eric waved goodbye and flew through the window, just as Mr Breakham managed to pick himself up. He immediately began bellowing,

"Come here, you ugly blighters! Come back to the orphanage!"

He looked around desperately. All the orphans had gone. All but Flora. He lunged at her clumsily, but she eluded him easily.

"We're all free! You'll never get us back in that smelly orphanage! Never!"

Breakham gave a cry of despair and flitted out of the house, still reeling with shock.

William didn't try to get away.

"Here, Flora, over here!" he called. He flew with Flora towards Roddy and Tessa who were still being flung round and round by the energy released from the spectral explosion.

"Grab our hands! Roddy! Tessa! Here, quick!" William yelled. He and Flora stretched out their hands for their friends to catch hold of. It was very difficult in the crazy swirl and mist of activity which was taking place.

"Quick!" William screamed.

With a terrific effort, he managed to grab Roddy's hand, while Flora seized Tessa's. Roddy and Tessa immediately became spectral.

"Yeah!" Flora cried.

But now there was a terrific *whooshing* sound.

"No!" Mrs Croker wailed above all the noise. "No!"

But it was too late. Both De-Sniff and Mrs Croker were sucked into and then swallowed by the swirling portal, which had opened in the ground. Roddy, Tessa, Flora and William also felt themselves being dragged towards it.

"Fly away from it!" William shouted to Flora. "Fly!"

But however hard they tried, a more powerful force was pulling them down at a phenomenal speed into the swirling, glowing chasm.

"Help!" Tessa screamed.

But it was no use. Like water spinning and swirling down a plug-hole, they were sucked into the gaping abyss. The next moment they were falling, dreamlike, through space and they had no idea if they'd live or die.

Chapter 22

Back to the Beginning

Down and down they tumbled and, after a few moments, landed like petals falling from a flower. They landed on a bridge and lay where they had fallen.

Roddy tried to get to his feet, but he was dazed and he felt strange.

"What ... what's happened?" Tessa whimpered. She was sitting in a heap, holding her head.

"I don't know," Roddy murmured. He shook himself to try and make his brain work. Then he stood up.

"What is it?" Tessa said, when she saw the contorted expression which crossed Roddy's face. "What's the matter?"

Tessa got up and stood next to him. She began to

realize that something very peculiar had happened. She and Roddy looked about them.

"This bridge." Tessa pointed.

"I know," Roddy said. "It crosses the same bit of river that we rowed over."

They now saw that the narrow little wooden bridge, which they were standing on, led up to Deadlock Hall.

"But it can't be!" Tessa cried.

William sat up and pushed back his cap.

"Blimey!" he called. He jumped to his feet and gazed all about him for a few seconds.

"That's the Hall ain't it?" Flora said.

"Yes," William said. "Deadlock Hall in all its glory."

The house was no longer derelict. It rose stupendously out of the rocky island. All the stone from which it was made was pale and clean and all its turrets shone brightly with copper. Flags flapped from the topmost towers. All the window-panes glistened in the sunshine. The road to it was neat and cared for. The gardens bloomed with flowers and shrubs. They could see gardeners at work. It was breathtakingly beautiful.

As the four of them stood gazing in wonder, a

coach with four horses pulling it came on to the bridge at the far end. They could hear the driver call, "Get on!"

And they felt the bridge shake as the coach moved towards them. As it came on, it went faster.

"It'll run us down!" Roddy shrieked. "There's no room!"

"Quick!" William cried. "Hold hands!"

As the children clutched their ghost friends' hands, the coach drove straight through the four of them.

They watched, as it wound its way up the side of the hill and went into the driveway of Deadlock Hall.

"Fings are coming back to me," William said quietly.

"What d'you mean?" Tessa said.

"I've seen that carriage before. It's the one what run me over and killed me." He stared at his friends.

Roddy and Tessa were gawping at him.

"You mean we're back in Victorian days?" Tessa said.

William nodded. "This is my time, this is."

"But what are we going to do?" Roddy whispered.

"I dunno, mate," William said, scratching his head. "We could start by finding me family."

"But…" Flora said. "How are we gonna get you two back to your own time? Eh?" She stared sympathetically at Roddy and Tessa.

Tessa felt her eyes begin to fill with tears, but she forced them back.

"There must be a way," she said bravely.

"Yes," Roddy said gently. "We'll just have to find it, that's all."